The Stablemaster's Heart

TALES OF LILLEFORTH
BOOK TWO

SARAH HONEY

Copyright © 2023 by Sarah Honey.

All rights reserved. This book or any portion thereof may not be reproduced or used in any manner whatsoever without the express written permission of the publisher except for the use of brief quotations in a book review.

This is a work of fiction. Names, characters, business, events and incidents are the products of the author's imagination. Any resemblance to actual persons, living or dead, or actual events is purely coincidental.

Edited by Jennifer Smith for LesCourt Author Services.

Cover Art by Steph Westerik Illustration.

stephwesterik.com

To Jessie and Ash. May your happy be ever after.

Author's Note

The author has chosen to use UK English in this book.

Contents

Chapter 1	1
Chapter 2	10
Chapter 3	23
Chapter 4	33
Chapter 5	41
Chapter 6	51
Chapter 7	62
Chapter 8	72
Chapter 9	83
Chapter 10	97
Chapter 11	108
Chapter 12	118
Chapter 13	131
Chapter 14	142
Chapter 15	156
Chapter 16	166
Chapter 17	177
Chapter 18	190
Chapter 19	201
Epilogue	211
Afterword	215
About the Author	217
Also by Sarah Honey	219

Chapter One

"Mice!"

Ollie squealed and jumped backward as a tiny creature spilled out of a split in the side of an old mattress, disturbed by the bed frame that had been thrown atop it.

Mother Jones laughed, entertained by the sight of his lanky stable lad leaping a foot in the air like a scandalised maiden. "They're only tiny, lad! Don't tell me you're afraid of a *mouse*?"

Ollie wiped his hands down the front of his shirt and jutted his chin out. "No! I see them all the time in the stables. I was just surprised, that's all. Who expects mattress mice?" He stepped close to the cart and, as if to show he wasn't afraid, shoved the bed frame more firmly into place on top of the mattress. No more mice emerged, and he let out a sigh of relief. "That's the last of it then?"

"Yes, lad. Now we just have to finish cleaning before the new groom arrives."

"When does he get here? Who is he? Do you know him?"

"Day after tomorrow, and no, I haven't met him. Chancell—*Prince Consort* Mattias hired him, and he comes from

Koroslova. That's all I know." Mother put his hands on his hips and turned his face up to the sun, stretching out his back. The cottage had been vacant since its previous occupant, Felix—Prince Consort Felix of Lilleforth, now—had abandoned it to go and stay in the castle with his lover the king, and it had taken Mother and Ollie most of the day to set it to rights. They'd wiped away cobwebs, removed the thick layer of dust that had coated every surface, scrubbed the kitchen clean, and taken out the old furniture, which Prince Felix had declared not up to standard. He'd been particularly insistent that the bed be replaced.

Apparently, it squeaked.

Ollie rubbed a forearm across his forehead, leaving a streak of dirt behind. He really had worked hard. He *always* worked hard, and Mother made a note to give him a day off once the new groom arrived. He was just about to send Ollie off for some hot water and a stiff bristled brush for the floors when Ollie's eyes widened. He straightened up and gasped out, "Your Highness!"

Mother turned and found Prince Felix sauntering towards them, his hands shoved into the pockets of an oversized coat. Underneath the coat, Felix was wearing an embroidered peacock blue doublet and fitted trousers, and he looked every inch a prince, which led Mother to suspect that perhaps he wasn't meant to be here.

"Sire," he said, ducking his head in a slight bow.

"Don't call me that," Felix said. "I'm still just Felix."

"That might be so, but you're also the prince consort. And that carries a title, sire."

Felix wrinkled his nose, but his expression brightened when he saw the cart full of old furniture ready to be hauled away. "So, you're done then?"

"Almost. Just the floors and a last clean through."

Felix wandered over and stuck his head in the cottage door. "It looks good. When does the new man arrive?"

"Day after tomorrow, sire. Prince Consort Mattias chose him, so I'm sure he's good at what he does."

"Either that, or he's a total disaster and Matty hired the lad to help him out, but hopefully he's actually competent." Felix's voice held the hint of a smile, and Mother couldn't deny that there was truth to what he was saying. The former chancellor was known for hiring people who needed help escaping a bad situation, although they usually turned out to be excellent at their jobs. He hoped that was the case here, because he could certainly use the help, having taken on the duties of caring for the royal mounts when Felix had moved to the castle. It occurred to Mother that this new groom would be the last person Mattias appointed before he moved to Evergreen with his new wife, the Princess Sophia.

It also occurred to him that today was the day of the farewell luncheon.

He cocked an eyebrow at Felix. "Speaking of which, isn't there an occasion that you're meant to be attending, *Highness?*"

Felix's brow furrowed again. "It's not fair," he grumbled, scuffing at the ground and dirtying the toes of his dress boots. "We avoided all the bollocks with our wedding by having a handfasting, but it turns out I *still* have to observe the etiquette of being a prince because apparently, it's a diplomatic faux pas not to have a big farewell for Sophia and Matty. I've had to be polite to guests for a *week*."

"Well, you did marry the king," Mother reminded him gently.

Felix's mouth curved up into a soft smile as he held out his left hand. The afternoon sunlight glinted off the band of gold there. "I did, didn't I?"

"So perhaps you need to accept that this is part of your life now, sire."

Felix's lips gave a rueful twist. "Perhaps I do. Still, it shouldn't be too difficult to adjust." He grinned. "I've been dealing with horseshit for years. This is just a different flavour. And it's worth it, for Leo." His expression went soft and dreamy like it always did at the mention of his new husband, and Mother envied him that, the ability to care so deeply for someone that he was willing to turn his whole world upside down.

As if summoned by the mention of his name, King Leopold of Lilleforth came around the corner into the small yard, his strides long and his expression set. "Felix!" he called, obviously impatient. "Are you still here? I swear to the gods, if you make us late for this luncheon, I'll put you over my knee and spank you pink, and not in the fun—" He broke off when he saw that Felix wasn't alone. "Oh."

"Sire," Mother said, ducking his head to hide his smile and pretending he hadn't heard a thing. He'd learned it was generally for the best where the king and his new husband were involved.

"Leo!" Felix said. "I was just coming to find you."

Leo raised a disbelieving eyebrow.

"I wanted to take one last look around the cottage before the new person moves in, and then I was coming right back, I swear." Felix took a step forward and peeled off his coat, revealing the formal dress underneath. "See? I'm ready. I just had to check the squeaky bed was gone."

For some reason, that had Leo's expression softening. "I suppose," he said, his tone fond. "Now come on, or else we really will be late."

He extended a hand and Felix took it, and they walked back up the track to the castle, the sound of soft laughter floating back on the breeze.

Ollie stared wide-eyed. "They're so in love," he said with a wistful sigh. He looked at Mother and tilted his head. "Have you ever been in love, Mr. Jones?"

"No, lad."

"Why not?"

"I've never had the time," Mother said, "what with running the stables."

It was mostly the truth. Mother wasn't a conventionally handsome man, not like the king with his strong jawline and piercing eyes, or Felix with his wavy hair and soft mouth, but he was tall and sinewy, with the muscles one would expect to gain from years of handling thousand-pound horses, and he had soft brown eyes, chestnut hair, and a slightly crooked smile that he had been told was charming more than once. He had no doubt that if he *did* want to attract someone into his bed, he'd have no trouble.

But Mother worked long hours as the stablemaster, overseeing the staff as well as providing hands-on care for the horses. By the end of the day, he was more interested in a warm meal and sleeping in his bed than bringing anyone into it.

Besides, nobody had ever...interested him that way. He could look at a person and know that they were pleasing to the eye, but he'd never had that driving desire to take it further, to feel someone else's hands on his skin, or their lips against his. And although he did think it would be nice to have someone to come home to, he wasn't driven by the need for physical affection.

"Mr. Jones?"

Mother was dragged out of his thoughts by Ollie, who was looking at him expectantly. "Shall I start on the floors?"

"Yes, lad. Go and fetch some hot water and we'll finish this. And after, shall you and I take Blackbird and Shadow out for a ride? They're well due."

Ollie's face lit up. "Really?"

"Really. You can take Blackbird." Ollie beamed, his eyes bright with excitement, and Mother smiled to himself. He knew that Ollie considered riding the king's horse to be a privilege of the highest order. "But only once the floors are done, mind, so you'd best get a move on."

Ollie nodded and scrambled to grab the water buckets, and Mother chuckled as he watched him run up the worn path that led to the laundry room, legs flying out behind him and buckets clanking.

Once Ollie returned he set to scrubbing with vigour, and it didn't take them long to finish up. The stone floors threw off a dull gleam when they were done, ready for the new furniture that was arriving tomorrow. Mother made a mental note to make sure that the cupboards were stocked with at least a few basics. He was sure the new groom would appreciate it.

Ollie tipped the grey water away down the drainage trough that ran behind the yard, and Mother clapped him on the back. "Well done, lad. Now, let's take those horses out, shall we?"

～

Mother loved nothing better than being on horseback. It gave a body a feeling of freedom that he'd never found anywhere else. The horses hadn't been properly ridden in days, what with the royal couple hosting guests, so Mother took the opportunity to give Shadow, Felix's mount, his head, with Ollie by his side on Blackbird. The horses made the most of the opportunity, their hooves eating up the miles as they raced along. The wind whipped through Mother's hair as he spurred his mount forward, and Ollie's cheeks were flushed, the boy laughing aloud as he rode. Even though Ollie was still in his teens, Mother could already tell he'd make a fine head groom someday. He had a solid work ethic, but more importantly, he had a passion for horses that Mother recognized as matching his own.

They rode in the afternoon sun, enjoying the ride and letting the horses set the pace until Mother's shirt was damp with sweat and his thighs ached. It was only when Shadow slowed, tossing his mane and blowing great hot breaths as they approached the woods that surrounded the castle, that Mother turned to head home. The sun was creeping lower in the sky, and the horses needed to be fed and tended to before it got dark.

It had taken some time for Felix to concede that he wouldn't be able to keep up his duties as royal groom, not while he was spending all his time with Leo at the castle learning the ins and outs of royal protocol. Eventually, though, he'd handed over the care of his horses to Mother, who had been happy to step into the role until a new groom was found.

Mother nudged Shadow along and Ollie did the same with Blackbird, and they rode back at a slow, steady pace. They reached the stables at the tail end of the afternoon, the approach of evening marked by soft pinks and oranges streaking the sky. Ollie insisted on grooming Blackbird since he was the one who'd ridden her, and it didn't take long before the horses were fed and settled in their stalls for the night. Mother gave an approving nod. "Good work. Now off you go and get your dinner."

"Are you coming to the kitchens?" Ollie asked. "They'll have leftovers from the fancy lunch."

Mother considered it but shook his head at the thought of the bustling, crowded tables and all those people. "Not tonight." He waved Ollie away. "I'll see you in the morning."

Ollie didn't need to be told twice, and once he'd gone Mother took the time to walk through the main stables, checking on the rest of the horses and making sure his other grooms had done their job. They had, of course. Mother ran a tight ship, and his staff knew better than to cut corners. He locked up the gates to the stable yard and started the walk back to his own cottage. Dusk had passed and it had turned into a still, clear evening. He could hear the faintest sounds of the ocean and on a whim, he turned and walked the other way, down the road that led through the town and towards the docks.

Mother had always loved the sea. Perhaps it had to do with the fact his father had been a fisherman. The smell of the ocean and the fresh bite of salt air on his cheeks made him feel alive, and he often wandered down to the docks of an evening.

He made his way down narrow, cobbled streets that smelled faintly of fish and past the market stalls. They were closed now, but early in the morning the street would be awash once again with fishwives, all displaying baskets of steely-eyed, glistening cod and pike, every one of them bellowing out assurances that *their* fish was the freshest and all claiming that they alone had the catch of the day.

Mother turned down one side street and then along another, rounding a corner and making his way to his favourite fish café, one that opened onto the street and did a decent dinner for a good price. Lamplight gleamed on the cobbles, and he settled himself at one of the outdoor tables. A round-faced lass bustled up to him with a nod and a smile. "Evening, Mr. Jones. The usual?"

"Please, Rosie. And a pint of cider."

He passed her a handful of coins and she disappeared. She was back a minute later with his drink and he took a long pull, savouring the crisp taste of apple as he gazed out over the gleaming black waters of the ocean, letting the quiet lapping of the waves wash over him.

There were people around, but it was a different sort of noise and bustle to that of the busy kitchens at the castle, and he settled in and watched them pass by. When Rosie brought his steaming hot cod in parsley sauce, it was just as good as it always was—which was to say, quite delicious, and better than anything he could have made for himself. He was glad he'd decided to buy his supper after the day he'd had cleaning out the cottage, and the long ride afterwards.

Still, at least they were ready for the new groom. Truth be told, Mother was looking forward to having an extra pair of hands about the place.

He just hoped that this groom lasted longer than the last one and didn't go running off and falling in love.

When his plate was empty, Mother hauled himself to his feet and drained his glass. He gave a nod to Rosie and then turned and started the walk home in the moonlight. It was a pleasant distance, his long, loping stride making short work of the road home, and soon enough he was opening the front door to his own cottage. He lit the lamps, bathing the room in a soft glow. Normally Mother found the solitude a relief after a day of chasing grooms and sorting out horses, but tonight the shadows emphasised the stillness and emptiness of the house, which was silent except for the thunk of Mother's boots hitting the floor as he peeled them off.

He sighed. Perhaps it was Ollie's talk of falling in love, or maybe it was seeing Leo and Felix so happy together, but the silence seemed particularly loud tonight. Sometimes—not often, but occasionally—he wished that he *could* find someone he was attracted to, just to have someone to share his space with. But he'd long accepted that he just wasn't built that way. He wasn't sure what that said about him, but it also wasn't something he pondered too deeply because he knew that no good ever came of pondering too deeply. Living and working at the castle, Mother had learned not to pass judgement on what was normal and what wasn't—and that included his own desires, or lack thereof.

Perhaps he'd bring home one of the kittens that seemed to be forever popping up around the place. There had been a litter born just last week in the barn—six of them, black and tiny and squirming, with scrunched-up noses and little pink toes and velvet soft ears. It might be nice, Mother reflected, to have a friendly face to greet him when he came home in the evening.

Even if that face did belong to a cat.

Chapter Two

Vasily Petrov, fourth son of the royal family of the kingdom of Koroslova, strode through the streets of Ravenport, tilting his head back to better inhale the salt of the ocean. Being this close to the sea was still a novelty, given that his home kingdom was completely landlocked, and he was enjoying it immensely. His rucksack bounced against his back in a heavy, thumping rhythm as he walked—unsurprising, since it currently held everything he owned. He'd moved out of his temporary lodgings this morning, and today was the day he started his new position as royal groom to King Leopold of Lilleforth.

He couldn't help the smile that split his face at the thought of having a job—a *real* job—for the first time in his life. That wasn't to say Vasily wasn't qualified for the position. He'd spent most of his childhood and teen years hiding out in the stables, ever since he'd been old enough not to get stepped on by an errant mount. When it had become obvious that he was becoming something of a fixture, the stablemaster had taken him under his wing, declaring that he might as well learn something useful. The man had trained him up just as he did all his other young grooms—the exceptions being that Vasily didn't have to shovel *quite* as much shit, and he was in no danger of getting a clip around the ears due to his royal status.

Vasily loved it. He'd initially started going to the stables to escape the endless obligation to act in a seemly manner and the disapproval that inevitably rolled off his father in waves when he failed to do so, and to get away from the teasing of his three older brothers. But as he grew older, it was mostly just because he'd grown to love spending time with the animals and the other grooms. He was sure his father thought it improper, the fourth son of the king spending his days in muck and straw, but Vasily had never been able to find it in himself to care.

It was just another thing that made him a terrible prince.

But Vasily had always felt that there was more to life than his royal position, and he'd long dreamed of exploring the world outside their own cloistered kingdom. So after careful thought, he'd chosen the week after his oldest brother and his wife had welcomed their first son into the world to ask permission to leave Koroslova and visit the surrounding countries.

He'd had all sorts of compelling arguments at the ready, but it had turned out to be unnecessary. Riding on a wave of good cheer at the continuation of his line, his father had barely put up any resistance, even though he'd initially scoffed at the idea.

"Travel?" King Alexei had snorted. "I don't really see the point of it. But then, there's not much point to you being here either, is there?"

"Alexei," Vasily's mother had chided. "Be nice. Why not say yes? It would be good for our boy to expand his horizons, explore other kingdoms for a year or so." She'd sent Vasily a knowing smile as his breath caught. A year? An *entire year*? It was more than he'd dared hope for.

But then, Queen Irina had always had a soft spot for her

youngest son. When he was little, she'd taken the time to sit with him and read him fairy tales and hadn't mocked him when he'd asked for the ones with the happy endings. And she knew of his desires, certainly—most little boys didn't ask if they'd get a handsome prince of their own—but it had always been their secret. And her support meant he'd almost certainly be granted permission to leave, because while it was true that his father ruled the kingdom, it was also true that he adored his wife and would give her anything she asked for.

Still, Vasily had wanted to dance for joy when his father had said, "I suppose," with a sigh. "At least it will get you out of the blasted stables."

His words had proved ironic, because ten days later Vasily's mother had informed him that she'd sent a letter to an old friend, and that to help start his journey, there was a position as royal groom waiting for him if he wished it—in Lilleforth.

Vasily's breath had caught, because *Lilleforth*.

His father had been vocal in his disapproval of Lilleforth, grumbling about "deviant behaviour" when the king there had recently married his groom. The marriage was the reason Lilleforth was the place Vasily was most curious about, but he'd never dreamed he'd get to visit.

It was inconceivable to him that there was a kingdom where being attracted to another man was acceptable, but it must be true. And if the king could take a husband, perhaps Vasily could safely explore his own urges, the ones he'd been hiding for all of his twenty-two years.

He'd never been able to deny what he felt. When he closed his eyes and took his cock in hand under the covers at night, he was more likely to be thinking about the way the sweat glistened on the blacksmith's skin by the light of the forge or the way the muscles in the man's forearms moved and bunched as he wielded his hammer than any pretty princess he might have been introduced to.

He'd taken the letter of introduction his mother had handed him, his fingers trembling. "But what will Father say? You know how he feels."

His mother had smiled, sharp and clever, and given a shrug. "I told your father I'd made some travel arrangements and that you'd be safe. He didn't express any interest in knowing the details, so I didn't tell him." Her smile had softened, and her tone had been warm when she'd said, "Go and explore, Vasily. Spread your wings. Find out who you are."

She'd always known him in a way that nobody else did.

Admittedly, Vasily had been confused at first as to why his mother had arranged for him to work as a groom, but she'd explained that working at the castle meant that Vasily would have a measure of protection. Only the people who mattered would know his identity. The understanding that passed between them—that it meant he was free to explore any inclinations he might have without being judged as the Prince of Koroslova—went unspoken.

It was oddly freeing being just Vasily, and he'd spent his first week in Ravenport lodging with a Mrs. Cully and exploring the city just because he could. It had been an experience. Nobody had bowed their head when he passed, and nobody had called him Your Highness, and he hadn't missed it. Of course, nobody had brought him all his meals or done his laundry for him either, and those things had been harder to figure out. But he'd muddled through, and at the end of the day, wasn't that the whole reason he was here? To learn about the world and how ordinary people lived in it?

He rolled his shoulders, making his backpack clank and clatter, and started the walk up to the castle.

∼

"That *can't* be your real name."

The words were out before Vasily could stop them. He clapped a hand over his mouth and the tall, lean man in front of him, the one who went by the unusual moniker of Mother Jones, pursed his lips. "It's what I've answered to my whole life, lad."

"No, I didn't mean...hells, I've been rude, haven't I? Oh, I'm *so* sorry. I just meant it's not exactly a common name, that's all, not that there's anything wrong with it. Hundreds of people are called Mother—no, thousands. More than that, even." Vasily flushed when he realized how stupid that sounded. "And now I'm babbling, and you probably think I'm a simpleton, but I promise I'm not. I'm just...nervous," he said with a sigh, his gaze dropping as he inwardly berated himself. He'd barely been here five minutes, and he was already making a mess of this.

The silence stretched out and when he dared lift his head, Mother was regarding him, his face set.

Well, that wouldn't do. Vasily might only be a fourth son and he might be terrible at formalities, but one thing he'd gotten very good at over the years was apologising. He took a deep breath, lifted his head, and squared his shoulders. "Can we please disregard everything I just said and start again? Hello, I'm Vasily, and I'm here to start work as the king's new groom. You must be Mother Jones. I'm so looking forward to working with you."

Mother tilted his head, considering, before the crease in his forehead disappeared. "It's fine, lad. You aren't the first to raise a brow at the name, and you won't be the last. Truth is, my mum had trouble filling in the birth certificate, and nobody checked before the christening, so here I am." His mouth quirked up in a crooked smile. "Mother Jones, at your service."

He extended a hand and Vasily stared for a second before he

remembered that he was meant to shake it. For all that Mother wasn't visibly muscular, Vasily could sense the underlying strength beneath his solid grasp, and something about it made his heart beat faster. The heat of Mother's touch lingered against his palm long after the man took his hand away, and Vasily found himself clenching and unclenching his fist in an effort to keep hold of the sensation as they walked along a rough stone pathway to a row of cottages.

Mother stopped at a door. "Here you go, lad. I cleaned it out personally, and there's a new bed and all, by order of the king."

Vasily stepped inside and looked around. The cottage was... tiny. Smaller than anywhere Vasily had ever stayed. It barely took five steps to cross the room to the wooden table, where he dropped his pack as he took in more of his surroundings. There was a bed and next to it a small table holding a lamp. There was another table and two wooden chairs, a small dresser that held a set of crockery, a wash basin, and a water jug. The stone floor was covered in a handmade rag rug, and there was another cushioned seat next to the hearth, which had been laid ready to light. It occurred to Vasily that he should probably learn to start a fire since he doubted anyone would be coming down from the castle to do it for him.

"It's..." Vasily looked around again. As small as the space was, it was clean and welcoming. Mother was watching him expectantly—and Vasily had been raised to be polite. "It's the nicest cottage I've ever stayed in," he declared. It wasn't a lie exactly.

Mother's face broke into a wide smile, exposing one crooked eyetooth, which Vasily found oddly endearing for reasons he couldn't quite parse. "It's a good position, the king's groom. I'll take you to meet Blackbird and Shadow, and then we'll go up to the kitchens and see what we can find for lunch."

Vasily nodded, excited at the prospect of getting to meet the horses. That was what he was here for, after all. Mother led him out of the cottage and along another path that went to the main stables. Vasily only got to glance inside as they passed, but he caught a glimpse of clean stalls and well-tended horses, the air redolent with the sweet scent of fresh hay. Mother was obviously good at his job, and it settled something in Vasily, knowing that he was working for someone who knew their business. He followed Mother, scurrying to catch up to his long strides, and they rounded a corner into a fenced yard that housed a smaller set of stables.

Mother paused outside the stable doors, picked up a nearby basket, and said, "Pick out a treat to introduce yourself with. The fastest way to Blackbird's heart is through her stomach."

Vasily peered into the basket. Inside was an assortment of fruits and vegetables—apples, carrots, quartered cabbages—and one lone potato. He bit his lip and picked it up, holding it out on his palm towards Mother. "No."

"No?" Mother raised his eyebrows.

Vasily hesitated. Perhaps they did things differently here. But then he shook off his uncertainty and squared his shoulders. "I don't know about you, but I was always taught never to feed a potato to a horse. Am I wrong?"

There was a stretch of tense silence, long enough for Vasily to second-guess himself and wonder if he'd offended Mother badly enough to get the sack before he'd even started. Then Mother's face split into a wide grin and he slapped Vasily on the back so hard that he staggered forward several inches. "Excellent! I told his Highness you'd know your onions! Or rather, your potatoes!"

"What?"

Mother laughed, a warm, rich sound. "The prince consort wanted to make sure you knew what you're about, since you were hired by the ex-chancellor—who's also a prince consort now, by the by. A man can't turn around without tripping over royalty these days. Anyway, Felix planted the potato in the basket to see if you'd notice."

Vasily had a feeling he should be offended. In all honesty, though, he was more pleased to hear that the prince consort cared so much about his horses. Although, given that he'd been their groom at one time, it only made sense that he'd want to make sure his replacement was up to scratch. He grinned at Mother and tossed the potato to him. "So I passed the test, then?"

"You passed." Mother gave him another crooked grin, and it sparked warmth in Vasily's chest.

The horses were gorgeous, and it was obvious they were well cared for just from their glossy coats and bright eyes. Vasily fed Shadow, the grey one, a chunk of carrot and rubbed his hands down his cheeks making soothing noises. Shadow echoed him with soft sounds of his own.

He moved on to Blackbird, who was breathtakingly beautiful. She nuzzled at his palm when he fed her an apple, and she didn't shy away at all when he ran his hands over her, getting a feel for her size. "That's my best girl," he murmured, standing in front of her and placing his palm on the side of her cheek. "Shall we be friends?"

Blackbird rewarded him by nuzzling at his face, startling a laugh out of him. He stepped back, wiping a sleeve over his face to get rid of the drool, and he was still grinning when Mother took him up to the kitchens.

"You can cook your own meals if you like, but there's always plenty of food in the kitchens if you'd rather not," Mother said as they approached the castle. Vasily thought of his one attempt to make porridge and the half-grey, half-black smouldering mess that had resulted and decided that he'd be making use of the kitchens.

Vasily stopped when the building came into view. The castle was an impressive sight, even to someone who'd grown up in a palace of his own, and he took a second to take in the wide gates and cobbled courtyard. Unlike his parents' palace, which was a long, low building of dark stone with little to no adornment, this castle towered high above him. The walls were the colour of bleached stone, and the castle boasted large windows and multiple balconies, with turrets rising up at intervals along the walls as if whoever designed it was just waiting for a fairy-tale princess to prick her finger on a spinning wheel somewhere.

"Impressive, isn't it?" Mother said, the pride in his voice unmistakable.

"It's lovely," Vasily agreed. He followed Mother along the road that led away from the front castle gates and around to a smaller, well-worn track that ran up the side of the castle. Vasily took the opportunity to study Mother as he strode alongside him. The man wasn't classically handsome, but he was *interesting* looking, and when he smiled, his features transformed into something warm and appealing.

Mother led him through a doorway and across a laundry room, and Vasily followed him through several long corridors until finally they stepped into the kitchens. It was a hive of activity and Vasily stood for a moment just soaking in the sounds and smells. It was exactly like the kitchens at home where Vasily liked to escape to sometimes. It was comforting in its familiarity, with people moving about in a well-choreographed dance as they ducked around each other carrying trays and jugs and slabs of meat and loaves of bread. His stomach grumbled, and Mother patted him on the shoulder. "Come on, let's find a seat."

Vasily nodded, following Mother to a series of long trestle tables and sitting in an empty spot. He stared around and Mother patted his shoulder again. "I'll be right back. Stay there."

Vasily watched as Mother sought out a small, pink-faced woman and started talking to her, his hands moving rapidly as he spoke. The woman nodded and went to one of the huge workbenches that were scattered around the room and started loading up two plates. Vasily could see chunks of salted pork, what looked like a hard cheese, and slabs of fresh bread topped with curls of butter. Mother said something that made the woman laugh as she handed him the plates, and then he was back, sliding the meal in front of Vasily. "There you go, lad."

"Thank you," Vasily said, savouring the novelty of someone handing him a meal and *not* calling him Highness. "This looks delicious."

"Cook knows what she's about." Mother nodded and started eating.

Vasily followed suit and he couldn't help the noise of appreciation that left him as he bit into the soft, warm bread and sharp cheese.

"What are you doing to that boy, Mother?" A young man slid into the seat next to Vasily. He had wavy brown hair, a wide grin, and his eyes sparkled with mischief. "You're new." He extended a hand to Vasily just as an older man sat next to him bearing two plates.

Vasily swallowed his mouthful and wiped his hand on his trousers before taking the proffered hand. "Yes. I'm Vasily. I just arrived."

The young man's face lit up with something like recognition. "Of course! You must be the—"

"—new groom from Koroslova," the older man said smoothly. "Of course." The young man opened his mouth to speak, and without missing a beat, his companion elbowed him in the ribs. "Welcome, Vasily."

"Majesties," Mother said, ducking his head in deference. "Vasily, this is King Leopold and his husband, Prince Consort Felix."

Vasily blinked.

This was the king and his husband? And they were eating *in the kitchen?* True, he'd had his own fair share of meals in the palace kitchens, but he was a fourth son and not very important at all. His father, on the other hand, would probably fade away to a shadow before it occurred to him to seek out the source of his meals. Vasily tried to imagine King Alexei sitting at a trestle table with a plate of bread and cheese. He couldn't quite manage it.

King Leopold was still looking at him expectantly, so he cleared his throat and managed to get out, "It's an honour to meet you both, sires." He wondered if he should kneel or bow or something. Was there protocol for casual kitchen lunches with royalty?

Prince Felix caught Mother's eye and said, "So. Did he pass?"

Mother grinned. "Aye, sire. Picked that potato right out of there. He's a good one."

"Oh, good! And stop calling me sire."

King Leopold raised an eyebrow over the slice of cheese he was eating. "What have you been up to, sweetheart?"

"His Highness wanted to be sure his replacement was up to snuff, sire," Mother said. "He's been testing young Vasily's knowledge."

The king rolled his eyes. "Yes, because Mattias was going to hire somebody unsuitable. Honestly, Flick."

Prince Felix shrugged. "I mean, he's not conventionally trained, is he?"

Vasily's hackles rose at that, and before he could stop himself, he snapped, "*He* is *right here*, thank you, and is perfectly qualified for the job."

As soon as the words left him, he slapped a hand over his mouth as if to stop his foot from wedging any farther in there.

Oh gods.

He'd managed to insult not just one royal, but *two*.

Felix stared at him wide-eyed, and for the second time that day, Vasily wondered if he'd be sacked before he even got to start, but Felix just threw back his head and laughed. King Leopold's face split into a wide grin. "Oh yes, you'll do wonderfully." He leaned in close as if imparting a secret. "Neither of us have any patience for milksops or bootlickers, and we don't stand on formality if we can help it. It's exhausting."

"You'd know," Felix said, "what with being a—"

"—*groom at the Koroslovan palace*," Leopold interrupted, giving Felix a pointed look.

"Yes, of course," Felix said. "What did you think I was going to say, *husband?*"

On hearing the word, the king's expression transformed into one of naked affection, and Vasily couldn't tear his gaze away as Leopold leaned in and pressed a soft kiss to Felix's cheek. His own mouth curled up in a smile at the sight.

Felix murmured something in Leopold's ear, and the king's eyes widened. He stood rapidly, lunch forgotten, as the legs of his chair scraped abruptly across the stone floor. "We, um. Business of state," Leopold said, his cheeks pink. "Nice to meet you, Vasily." And then he was hurrying across the kitchen, dragging his young husband by the hand.

Vasily watched them go.

"Aye," Mother said. "Mad for each other, they are." He turned to Vasily. "What about you? Is there a nice lass waiting at home?"

Vasily shook his head. "No." He hesitated, unsure whether he should say more. But, he decided, he *was* meant to be spreading his wings—and he couldn't do that without ruffling some feathers. So he took a deep breath and added, "I'm more interested in nice young men, actually."

It was the first time he'd admitted out loud that he preferred the company of men, and he waited with bated breath, bracing himself.

Mother, though, just shrugged. "Fair enough. I'm sure you'll find plenty of willing lads working around the castle. All I ask is that if it's my grooms, you don't bugger them too vigorously. I need them fit to work."

And with that he took his empty plate and walked away, leaving Vasily staring after him. He wasn't sure what reaction he'd been expecting, but that wasn't it.

Chapter Three

Vasily Petrov was a puzzle.

Mother couldn't quite put his finger on what it was about his new groom, but there was something odd about him.

The lad really did know his horses, and in the week that he'd been here, he'd already proven himself an asset, but at the same time, he seemed clueless about some of the simplest things.

For example, he always took his meals in the kitchens. Mother wasn't sure if he couldn't cook or just preferred not to, but three times a day, Vasily trekked over to the castle to eat.

His second morning at the castle, he'd looked most put out as he'd explained that the fire that had taken him forever to light the night before had barely lasted any time at all. When Mother had asked if he'd banked it properly, he'd responded with a blank stare.

Mother had made sure to stop by that evening and set the hearth up to last through the night. Part of him had worried Vasily might be offended at Mother assuming he was ignorant, but on the contrary, he'd beamed at Mother, thanking him profusely.

He'd never played a hand of cards, but watched in fascination as the other grooms dealt and folded and bet their pennies while he asked questions about *why* two red cards were better than two black ones, and what did four of a kind mean?

And just yesterday he'd asked Mother if someone would be coming by to clean his cottage any time soon. Mother hadn't replied, just raised an eyebrow, and after a few seconds, understanding had dawned on his face. Vasily had blushed a deep red, ducking his head and mumbling, "Of course. I'm meant to do those things myself, aren't I?"

It wasn't that Vasily didn't know how to work hard. His long days in the stables had proven that. It was more like he didn't know how to take care of *himself*.

It had prompted Mother to ask, "Who looked after you back home, lad?"

"Oh, um. We had people who did all that," Vasily had said, eyes still downcast. "It wasn't like here." He hadn't shared further, and Mother hadn't pried. Vasily was one of Mattias's, after all.

Perhaps his being here had something to do with his confession that he preferred the company of men. Mother didn't know much about Koroslova, but he did know that there were some things they were firmly against, and that was one of them.

Regardless, Vasily was a mystery wrapped in an enigma wrapped in a horse blanket—but despite that, Mother couldn't help but like him. He was a pleasure to work with, genial and well-mannered, and always ready with a smile or a joke, his soft, lilting voice often echoing through the stables as he hummed while he worked.

More than once this past week, Mother had found himself humming along.

If anything, Vasily was almost *too* charming. With his shoulder-length golden hair that he kept pulled back and tied in place with a leather thong, his broad muscular chest, and his enchanting accent, he was the newest darling of the palace staff. Today was the second time this week Mother had rounded the corner into the stable yard to find a gaggle of kitchen girls staring transfixed as Vasily told them tales of his home country.

When he saw Mother, Vasily nodded at him and said, "Mr. Jones is here, and so I must go back to work, ladies," while pressing a hand to his heart. Most of the girls scattered, giggling and whispering behind their hands. One or two showed signs of lingering but were soon dissuaded when Vasily picked up a shovel and started to muck out the stalls.

"You could just tell them to get back to work," Mother pointed out once the last of the doe-eyed lasses had departed. "They've all got better things to do than be hanging around the stables."

"They weren't here for long," Vasily said. "Besides, they're just being friendly."

Mother let out a sigh and pondered whether Vasily had grown up under a rock. "Lad, they're *flirting*."

Vasily stared at him, eyes wide with shock. "Are they?"

Mother cast his gaze heavenward. "Course they are."

"Why on earth would they do that?"

Mother wondered at Vasily's obliviousness. He wasn't interested in that sort of thing himself, but even he could see that Vasily had a certain exotic appeal, with his hair and his accent and his bright eyes and brighter smile. "Well," he said. "It's. You're." He cleared his throat, dragging the toe of his boot through the dirt. "They're taken with you, aren't they? You're charming, lad, and handsome to boot."

Vasily's face broke into a delighted, if somewhat shocked, smile. "Am I?" It was as if nobody had ever told him he was attractive before.

Maybe they hadn't.

For reasons he couldn't quite name, Mother was saddened to think that Vasily was genuinely unaware of his own appeal, so he raised his gaze from the dirt, caught Vasily's gaze, and said firmly, "A face like yours *and* a job at the castle? You're a catch, lad. I daresay you could have any young man you wanted, if you set your mind to it. Why not find someone who takes your fancy and try flirting yourself?"

Vasily's cheeks stained pink against his pale skin. "I...I could," he said, almost wonderingly. His smile widened. "I *could*, and nobody would care, would they? Not in Lilleforth."

He beamed like he'd just been handed the key to a chest of unknown treasures.

Vasily continued to smile to himself all afternoon as he polished the tack and swept the stables and cleaned the horses' hooves and filled the feed troughs, and that smile made something warm bloom in Mother's belly.

He hoped the lad *did* find someone to flirt with, because Mother got the feeling Vasily hadn't been able to do so openly before.

At the end of the day after the stables has been closed up for the night, Mother joined Vasily in the walk up to the castle for their dinner. "I've heard it's beef and ale pie tonight." It was a favourite of his, and he smiled at the thought.

They sat down with their pies at the long, crowded table, and Mother watched as Vasily exchanged nods and greetings and snippets of conversation with the other staff who were sharing a meal. Vasily had a talent with people, and he seemed perfectly at home after just a week. Mother couldn't help but envy his easy manner and charm. If Vasily ever did find someone to flirt with, Mother was sure he'd be devastatingly good at it.

But Vasily didn't seem inclined to linger after his meal was finished. He turned down an invitation from some of the others to go into town, yawning and pleading tiredness, and Mother joined him. Vasily was unusually quiet on the walk back to the cottages.

"Not a fan of the pies, lad?" Personally, Mother couldn't think of a single thing not to like about a good pie.

"Oh no, they were lovely. It's just..." He stopped walking and turned to Mother. "I can't cook." His shoulders hunched at the admission. "I wish I could. Then I could fend for myself and not have to face a kitchen full of people. Not that I don't like everyone here," he hastened to add. "I'd just like to be able to"—he shrugged— "stay home and roast an egg or something."

Vasily sighed and trudged along the path, and Mother found himself throwing an arm over his shoulders as they walked. The lad had broad shoulders, but Mother had a long enough reach that Vasily fitted quite perfectly against his side. Vasily leaned into the touch. "I have bad news, lad," Mother said. "You don't roast eggs. You boil 'em."

Vasily gasped, looking positively betrayed, and Mother fought back a smile.

"Tell you what. I'm sure Cook or one of the girls in the kitchen would be happy to teach you some of the basics."

Vasily shook his head. "I wouldn't inflict it on them. The last time I tried making porridge, I burnt the entire arse out of a pot. Cook chased me down the hallway with a wet dishrag and banned me from the pal—the kitchens."

Mother chuckled at the mental image. "Ah well, we've all done something like that. First time I tried to cook, I blackened a haddock and filled the entire house with smoke." He smiled at the memory. "I was twelve, I think."

"Oh no, I wasn't a child when I burnt the porridge," Vasily said with a wry twist of his mouth. "This was last month."

Mother couldn't help but laugh out loud at that, and Vasily joined him. His laugh was rich and deep, echoing through the night air, and by the time they reached the door of Vasily's cottage, his customary cheerful smile was back in place.

He stepped out from under Mother's arm, where he'd remained tucked against him for the entire walk back, and opened his door. The cottage was in darkness. Before he could disappear inside, Mother said, "There's a place down at the docks where I go some nights that does a nice fish supper. You could join me next time I go, if you wanted a change from the kitchens." He wasn't even sure why he was asking except that he liked Vasily and he was new to the city, and showing him around seemed like the decent thing to do.

Vasily paused with the door open and gave a small, bashful smile. "That would be nice. I've found that I'm quite fond of fish."

"We'll do that, then." Mother gave a slight nod and walked away, his breath fogging the air as he walked. When he entered his own cottage and saw the embers glowing in the hearth, waiting to be stoked back to life, a thought struck him. There had been no embers in Vasily's hearth. Odds were his fire had gone out, and he was probably desperately trying to get it started again. The sigh he gave was fond as he carefully scooped some coals into a bucket and, cradling it gently, went back to Vasily's cottage and rapped on the door.

Vasily pulled the door open a few inches, his hair hanging loosely round his face where he'd let it out of its ponytail, his shirt untucked. "Yes?"

Mother blinked. "Sorry, lad. I didn't think you'd be getting undressed."

Vasily looked down at himself. "Oh no, it's fine." He tucked his shirt in hastily and opened the door wider. "Did you need something?"

"I wondered if you needed a hand with the hearth," Mother said, shifting from foot to foot and holding the bucket out. "I'm guessing it went out again."

Vasily ran a hand over the back of his neck, ducking his head. "Will you think me hopeless if I say yes?"

"Not at all, lad. I suspected as much, so I brought some coals over to get it going." Vasily stepped aside to let him in. The warmth flooding him at Vasily's pleased smile was a direct contrast to the chill that was seeping out of the stone walls.

He crouched in front of the hearth and made short work of starting the fire, being sure to show Vasily what he was doing every step of the way, instructing him on how to add the fuel just so and how to bank the coals so it could be easily revived in the morning. Vasily nodded, his brow creased in concentration as he added another small log. "I'm sure I'll get the hang of it this time," he said. "I just forgot this morning. At home, the maids would do it for me." He rubbed his hands together and held them out towards the flames, the firelight illuminating the shadow of his jawline and making his eyes gleam.

"Oh? Well off, were you?"

Vasily tensed. "You could say that," he said, carefully neutral, and Mother knew not to press further.

He turned his attention back to the fire, prodding it with the poker. "Well, you'll get the hang of it soon enough. Maybe I'll teach you to cook as well, and you'll be roasting eggs in no time."

That earned him a laugh and Vasily relaxed again. "Maybe we'll start with bread and cheese."

"Maybe." Mother stood from where he'd been crouched in front of the hearth, his knees cracking, and put his hands in the small of his back, leaning back and stretching his muscles. Vasily made a small noise, and Mother turned to find him staring fixedly into the flames, his cheeks pink. Good. It meant the cottage must be getting warm.

He was oddly reluctant to leave, but he didn't have any reason to linger. "Well, I'll be off. Don't forget His Majesty and His Highness are riding early in the morning."

"I won't," Vasily said, swallowing and still staring at the flames. "Thank you for the coals."

"You're welcome, lad. Come and see me any time you need warmed up." Vasily made a choked sound at the same moment

Mother realized exactly how that had sounded. "For *coals,* I mean. For the fire."

Vasily finally turned to look at Mother, the corners of his mouth twitching with amusement. "Of course."

Mother gave a nod and left before he embarrassed himself further.

∽

The next morning there was a knock at Mother's door just as he was dressing. It was far too early for visitors, and his first thought was that there was some sort of emergency, but when he opened the door, shirt still unlaced and trousers untied, it was to find Vasily on his doorstep, cheeks pink from the cold. He was carrying the bucket Mother had left there the night before and nestled inside was a cluster of glowing coals. Vasily held it out as if seeking approval. "I did it!" he said, his excitement obvious. "I kept it going!"

Mother ran a hand through his sleep-mussed hair, and Vasily looked so pleased with himself he couldn't help but smile, caught up in his enthusiasm. "Good job, lad!"

Vasily continued to hold the bucket out.

Mother reached out, confused. "And you've brought these to me because…"

Vasily rolled his eyes. "Well, to replace the ones I used, obviously. That's just good manners."

Mother bit back a smile. "They're coals, Vasily. You can keep them. I have plenty."

Vasily pulled the bucket back towards him hesitantly. "You're sure?"

"I promise." Mother stepped aside and extended a hand. "Come inside and check for yourself."

Vasily stepped over the threshold, looking around the room with ill-disguised curiosity. "Oh, it's bigger than mine."

"That's not the first time I've heard that," Mother said—and where had *that* come from? It had almost sounded like he was… flirting. Except Mother didn't flirt.

He decided he'd blame the early morning and the fact he hadn't eaten yet, and hope Vasily didn't notice.

Luck was on his side. Vasily was still caught up in looking around as he carried the bucket over to the hearth and set it down. His nose twitched at the scent of food wafting from the pot where Mother had set his breakfast to cook earlier while he'd been getting dressed.

Mother tied the laces on his shirt and trousers and pulled two bowls off the shelf, dishing up a scoop of porridge into each. After a moment's thought, he fished out a small jar of honey from the cupboard and drizzled a generous dollop over the top of both bowls, setting them down on the table. "You might as well join me for breakfast, save yourself the walk up the hill."

"Please." Vasily gave one of his sunshine smiles and sat at the table. "Oooh, this smells good."

Mother fetched them spoons and settled across from Vasily. It was nice, having company while he ate, and Mother didn't even mind when their knees banged together under the small table.

Soon enough the bowls were empty, and Vasily hummed contentedly as he licked the last traces of honey off the back of his spoon. "There's more if you want," Mother offered.

Vasily shook his head. "I have to get the horses saddled up. The royal couple will be here for their ride soon enough. But thank you. It was nice." He tapped the side of his bowl with his spoon in an irregular rhythm before saying, "Um, maybe… maybe we could do this again? If you taught me how, I could even cook for you. We could take turns."

The idea was more appealing than it had any right to be, and

Mother found himself nodding. "We could do that. You'd have to learn to boil water first, mind."

Vasily grinned. "I could work my way up to a roast egg."

Mother laughed loudly, and warmth settled in his chest. It would be nice to have Vasily visiting regularly, with his ready laughter and easy smile, and Mother was confident he'd soon have Vasily making porridge with the best of them. Even if Vasily *was* currently as much of a disaster in the kitchen as he claimed, Mother had spent years training a variety of stable boys and grooms in equine care, and he liked to think he was good at teaching.

Surely he could teach one man to boil an egg?

Mother wondered again what sort of upbringing Vasily had had that he'd missed out on learning the everyday things like building a fire and feeding himself—not that it mattered where he came from. He was here now, and Mother was happy to help fill in the odd gaps in Vasily's knowledge.

In fact, he looked forward to spending more time with Vasily, because he was *fun*, and Mother suspected that, despite the difference in their ages and backgrounds, they could be good friends—maybe even *best* friends.

And for reasons he couldn't quite parse, Mother wanted that.

Chapter Four

"You certainly take good care of my boy."

"Thank you, sire," Vasily said, glowing with pleasure under the praise. Prince Felix ran a hand down Shadow's cheek. The horse whinnied his pleasure and nuzzled his owner, his nostrils flaring in hopes of sniffing out a treat.

"Don't call me that, Vasily. You've got more royal blood in you than I'll ever have." Felix produced a chunk of apple for Shadow and held it flat on his palm.

"Not here, sire," Vasily said. "Here, I'm just the groom."

"And are you enjoying it, being a—" Felix wrinkled his nose. "I was going to say commoner, but that sounds insulting."

"Untitled?" Vasily suggested with a smile. In the three weeks since his arrival, he'd gotten to know the rulers of Lilleforth better, and he'd formed something of a bond with Felix, charmed by his irrepressible humour and disregard for all things proper. Vasily's insistence on calling him sire wasn't only because it was right and proper. It was also because Vasily knew it made Felix squirm.

"I suppose," Felix said. "Anyway. How is it? Any regrets? No desire to go running back to Koroslova to be waited on like a prince?"

"None at all, sire," Vasily said, grin widening. And it was true. His muscles ached from doing more physical labour than he was used to, and he missed the feather beds at the palace and someone running him a bath every night. But he didn't miss the rest of it.

"Good. It's hard to get decent help these days, and you're a bloody good groom." Felix petted Shadow's neck and walked out into the stable yard, peering at the sky. "It looks like rain. I hope Leo hurries up."

"I'm sure he'll be here directly, sire." A voice came from the doorway, and Vasily perked up and turned to greet its owner.

"Hello, Mother!" Even though Vasily had only seen the man an hour ago when they'd shared lunch, he warmed at the sight of him, all long limbs and tousled hair with stray bits of straw clinging to his shirt like he'd been rolling in the hay.

Thoughts of Mother rolling in the hay made certain other parts of Vasily perk up, but he tamped those thoughts down *hard*. Mother was a fine, strong specimen of a man, true, and Vasily certainly found him appealing—truth be told he'd already featured in more than one of Vasily's dreams—but Mother was his friend, and it was obvious that he wasn't interested in Vasily like that.

They *were* friends, though.

Mother had made good on his promise and taken Vasily down to the docks one evening and treated him to a delicious fish supper while pointing out which food stalls to avoid if he didn't want a sour stomach the next day. They'd lingered over cider, talking and watching the waves roll across the ocean until it had started to get chilly. Vasily, who'd somehow worked his way through four pints of cider, had been pleasantly tipsy by the time they'd walked back to the castle, with Mother supporting his weight for at least half the way.

The next morning Vasily had woken with a pounding head and a roiling gut, and it was while he'd been praying for a quick death that Mother had appeared at Vasily's door. He'd chuckled at the state of him, but he'd also presented Vasily with a headache powder and several slices of thick fruit cake, insisting it would settle Vasily's stomach. For a wonder, it had worked, and Vasily could have kissed him.

Out of gratitude, of course. Nothing else.

They'd also started sharing breakfast most days. Under Mother's patient tutelage, Vasily could now produce a porridge that was *almost* entirely edible if you ate around the lumps.

Mother gave him a nod and a smile. "Afternoon, Vasily. Mounts all ready?"

"Of course they are," Felix said, "because your man knows his job."

"That he does," Mother agreed with a grin. "And he's a lot more reliable than my last groom. That lad disappeared up to the castle at the drop of a hat."

Felix's eyes danced with merriment, and his mouth curved up in a smile. "Be fair. There was an attraction at the castle that was nigh irresistible."

"Did I hear you call me irresistible? How very flattering, sweetheart," King Leopold said, striding into the stables. He came to a stop next to Felix and pressed a kiss to his cheek. "Sorry I'm late. I was in a meeting with the council, but I'm all yours now."

"Yes, you are," Felix said, his smile widening, and he and Leo led their horses out into the yard. Felix murmured something in the king's ear that made Leo bellow with laughter and slap Felix's arse playfully before they mounted up and rode off.

Vasily hooked his elbows over the stable yard fence and watched them depart, his chest tightening with something like envy at the obvious attraction between the two. Maybe he could have that someday—just as soon as he worked up the nerve to ask anyone on a date, or even flirt with them. It was, he was discovering, easier said than done.

He was almost certain one of the guards had been eyeing him up, but it was hard letting go of a lifetime of hiding who he was and what he liked. He *wanted* to ask Jeremy, the guard in question, if he'd like to go for a pint at the tavern one evening. But what if he *did* ask, and Jeremy said yes? What then?

"They're a good match." Mother's voice broke into his thoughts, and Vasily turned to find him nodding in the direction of the horses as they grew smaller on the horizon, Leo's laughter floating back on the breeze. "They're lucky to have found each other."

Vasily nodded and gave a sigh.

Mother quirked an eyebrow. "Something on your mind, lad?"

Vasily considered saying nothing for a moment. But Mother had proved to be a wealth of information on anything and everything, and he'd been nothing but kind so far. Maybe he'd have some advice about this as well.

"It's—" Vasily kept his gaze fixed on the horizon. "*How*, though?" he burst out. "How did they find each other? How do you know if someone is interested, or if you're imagining it?"

"Ah," Mother said. "Someone you've got your eye on, lad?"

Vasily bit his lip and reminded himself that Mother had never judged him—and besides, he'd asked. "Maybe. There's a guard that I think might like me. But I don't know what to do next or if I'm imagining it. How, exactly, do I ask someone out? What if I ask and they say no? What if they say *yes?*"

Mother gave a low chuckle and draped an arm over Vasily's shoulders, the gesture familiar and comforting. "You're asking the wrong person, lad. I've never been much for romance and attraction or any of that. But I will say, if it's young Jeremy, you're not imagining it. I don't believe that lad had seen the inside of the stables before you arrived, but he's been down here two days this week already."

"Oh!" Vasily's mood brightened instantly at the thought that someone—*anyone*—was interested in him. "Are you sure?"

Mother gave him that crooked smile that Vasily was becoming so fond of. "What was his reason for coming last time, remind me?"

"He said he needed some straw? It was for the stove in the guards' quarters."

"A handful of straw for the stove in the guards' quarters, right. And why was he here the time before that?"

Vasily's brow creased as he tried to remember. "He said...he was familiarising himself with the stables in case there was an emergency?" Come to think of it, he'd thought it odd at the time, given that if the king or his husband ever needed an escort, it was always Captain Hobson or the physically imposing but good-humoured Thomas, who had replaced Felix as Leopold's personal guard.

"He lingered so long making small talk with you that the captain sent someone to fetch him, as I recall." Mother shook his head and let out a soft chuckle, the arm around Vasily's shoulders tightening for a moment. "He's sweet on you, lad. Or at least, he wants to be."

Vasily's face heated. "Oh. That's—" He swallowed. "That's mildly terrifying, actually."

Mother pulled away and turned to look at him, brow furrowed. "You just said you like him. And he likes you back. Surely that's a good thing?"

Vasily slumped against the rails. "Yes. No. I don't know."

"Ah." Mother nodded sagely. "I'm glad we cleared that up."

Vasily raised his head just enough to see Mother grinning, his expression mocking him gently, and the smile on his face was enough to unknot the ball of nerves in his stomach at least a little. One of the many things Vasily liked about Mother was how easy it was to talk to him. Vasily propped his elbows on the railing and rested his chin. "I'm not good at"—he gestured vaguely with one hand— "flirting. Courting. Any of it. I haven't ever had the chance. And I'm terrified that if I invite Jeremy for a pint, he'll think it *is* just for a pint and be offended if I suggest anything more. Or worse, he'll think I want to—"

Fuck, he didn't say, unable to force the word out.

"To spoon?" Mother suggested, and Vasily could have sworn his cheeks held a tinge of pink.

"Spoon," Vasily agreed, all the air leaving him in a whoosh.

"And do you?" Mother asked. "Want to spoon someone?"

Vasily's lungs constricted at the thought. He ran his palms over his face and let out a groan. "Maybe? But I've never spooned anyone before. I haven't, um, dabbled in cutlery at all, really."

Mother's hand came to rest on his shoulder again, broad and comforting. "I'm sure you'll figure it out, with the right help."

"Yes, but it's the *getting there,*" Vasily said. "I can't even tell when someone is flirting. How am I meant to know if they're trying to seduce me? And how am I meant to seduce *them*?" He heaved another sigh. "Perhaps I'll follow your lead and stick to horses. People are too complicated."

Mother patted his shoulder, and his expression grew serious. "You didn't leave your home to travel just so you could spend the evenings alone, lad. This is your chance to do things you'd never do back in Koroslova, right?"

Vasily swallowed. Mother was right. He'd been given a gift— an entire year—and it would be a shame to squander it, but still. "I don't know what to say or do, though. Why didn't my tutors teach me something useful, like how to talk to attractive people?" he said, sounding pitiful even to his own ears. "Why can't everybody be easy to talk to like you?"

Mother's brow creased. "Me?"

"Yes, you. You don't say I'm stupid because I don't know

how to bank a fire, and you don't think I'm a"—he swallowed again, feeling his face heat—"a deviant, just because I prefer the company of men." He wrinkled his nose. "At least, I *think* I prefer it. But at the rate I'm going, I'll never find out because I'm too scared to say hello, let alone anything else."

Mother's mouth pursed and his grip on Vasily's shoulder tightened before he spoke, low and serious. "First off, lad, who you prefer to keep company with isn't anybody else's business, and I'd like to see anyone *dare* to call you that when I'm around."

His words made Vasily's heart flutter in his chest for reasons he chose not to think about.

"Secondly," Mother continued, softer now, "you're being too hard on yourself. This 'asking people to keep company' lark is all new to you. I'll bet you couldn't tack up a horse the first time you tried, either."

That drew a smile out of Vasily as he remembered his first failed attempt at putting on a bridle. "Oh, that was a disaster. The straps were all arse about face, and I ended up tying the thing in knots before the head groom took it off me."

Mother smiled knowingly. "Aye, I've seen that happen a time or two. But you can get a horse saddled up and ready to ride quick as a flash now, right?"

"Well, yes, but that's only because I've had lots of practice."

"Well then, you'll just need to practice this as well." Mother ruffled his hair, and Vasily leaned into the touch without thinking about it. Mother's hand stilled and he gazed at Vasily, his brow creasing as though he were considering something. He drew his hand away, jutted his chin out and, voice rough, said, "Course, you could always practice on me."

Vasily blinked. "What?"

Mother ducked his head. "You said you wished you knew how to talk to attractive men. Well, I'm no handsome young buck like Jeremy, but I daresay I'd do well enough if you want to learn how to give a compliment without making a tit of yourself."

"Oh no," Vasily said without thinking. "You are, actually. Handsome, I mean. For your age," he added quickly, to distract Mother from the fact he'd just said he found him attractive. His cheeks flamed as he berated himself.

Shut up shut up shut up.

Mother's head snapped up, but he didn't look upset, more surprised. He raised an eyebrow. "Oh? Handsome for my age, am I? How old do you think I am?"

"Um..." Vasily scrambled to think of a number that seemed realistic. In truth, he hadn't given it much thought. "Forty-two?"

Mother fixed him with a look. "Cheeky little shit! I'm bloody well thirty-five. And even I know that the rule is when someone asks how old they look, you shave off ten years."

"Oh. Sorry," Vasily said, biting his lip. Now that he looked closer, he could see that Mother was indeed younger than he first appeared—it was his height, his tanned skin, and his work-rumpled clothing that made him seem older at first glance. "So, I should say you look…thirty-two?"

"Now you're getting it." Mother grinned. "Don't worry, lad. We'll make a smooth talker out of you yet."

Chapter Five

Mother sat alone in his cottage that night, staring at the wall as he tried to work out what had come over him.

Why had he offered to let Vasily learn to flirt with him? What had he been *thinking?*

In truth, he knew exactly what he'd been thinking. It was the same thing he'd been thinking when he'd taken Vasily a bucket of hot coals, and when he'd invited him to breakfast every day, and when he'd brought him a headache cure and Cook's special hangover cake after Vasily had gotten drunk.

Vasily needed someone to take care of him.

Of course, it wasn't the first time Mother had looked after his grooms. It was just that normally it was the younger stable boys that needed a guiding hand, with some of them away from home for the first time and in need of a parental figure.

With Vasily, it was different. Mother's feelings towards him were…well, they were complicated.

And most definitely *not* parental.

Mother *liked* Vasily. From a professional standpoint, there was nobody who worked harder. He appreciated his easy smile and quick wit and the way he hummed unfamiliar, lilting tunes as he worked. But Mother was finding that, as he spent time with Vasily and their friendship grew, he was starting to notice things about Vasily that he never had before.

For example, there was the way his face lit up like a sunbeam as he plucked dandelions and wove them into a hasty flower crown, draping it over the hair of whoever was closest. Sometimes he stood on his tiptoes, grinning, and bestowed a crown on Mother. And Mother, for his part, kept every single one of them pressed flat between the pages of a book in his bottom drawer for reasons he couldn't quite articulate.

Then there was Vasily's recently developed habit of stripping off his shirt as he worked, unused to the heat—even though the temperatures were mild at best. Mother wasn't going to stop him. Vasily came from a cold climate, and the last thing Mother wanted was his new groom laid up with heatstroke. But the last time Vasily had stripped, Mother hadn't been able to stop staring at his broad muscled chest with its thatch of dark blond hair, and it had made his stomach swoop and dive in unfamiliar ways that, despite their newness, weren't entirely unpleasant.

It was only later that night in bed, when he'd closed his eyes and the vision of Vasily, bare-chested and glowing with a light sheen of sweat, had his cock hardening, that Mother had finally identified what he felt as attraction—which in and of itself was unexpected, but even more so because Vasily was a *man*.

Mother had always assumed that if he ever did feel a physical pull towards someone it would be a woman, but apparently nobody had told his cock that. And although it had been something of a surprise to realise where his preferences lay, his initial moment of shock hadn't lasted. Mother had been too busy wondering what it would be like to run his hands down Vasily's broad chest or kiss the jut of his collarbones, or perhaps plunder that smiling mouth. The very idea of it had been enough that he'd ended up taking himself in hand and working himself to completion, panting Vasily's name into the quiet of the night.

So yes, complicated.

But he *was* fond of Vasily, and he did want to help him. And because Vasily was clueless, that had led to Mother presenting himself like a training yard dummy for Vasily to use to hone his romantic aim, so to speak.

Vasily might not be interested in Mother, but if he wanted to dally with one of the lithe young guards that marched around the castle—all handsome in their smart doublets and long, polished boots, short swords at their hips—then Vasily should get whatever he wanted. Even though, in Mother's opinion, Vasily could do much better than Jeremy, who was a muttonhead.

He wondered again what Vasily's background was. Mother had noticed that he rarely mentioned his family, and he hoped the poor boy hadn't been sent away, that his family hadn't been cruel to him—although he couldn't see how *anyone* could be cruel to Vasily. It would be like kicking a puppy.

Still, Vasily seemed happy with his lot here in Lilleforth working as a groom, even though he'd obviously had a wealthy upbringing. Mother hoped that it had been his choice to exchange wealth for the freedom to explore who he was.

He sighed, standing and stretching his arms over his head just as there was a soft tap on the door. When he opened it, Vasily was standing there, his usual smile tinged with uncertainty. "Hello, Mother."

The very sight of him had Mother smiling, and he was struck once again with the knowledge that he found Vasily attractive. He ducked his head to hide the blush he could feel climbing his cheeks as he stepped aside to let him in. "Hello, lad. Have you come to walk up for supper with me?"

Vasily swallowed, his hands tugging at the hem of his shirt, his own cheeks blazing. Mother wondered what had him shuffling from foot to foot like he'd stepped in a nest of ants. "I, um. I wondered if I could take you down to Rosie's for a fish supper? My treat."

Mother found himself ridiculously pleased at the unexpected invitation, even though he knew it was probably just part of Vasily's courting practice. A fish supper did sound nice. "That'd be just the thing," he said, and Vasily's smile became more genuine.

They walked side by side down the path to the docks, the full moon lighting their way and illuminating the puffs of warm breath that escaped them in tiny clouds. Mother rubbed his hands together before tucking them under his armpits to chase away the chill. "It's a brisk one," he said, eyeing up Vasily, who wasn't even wearing a coat. "Aren't you freezing?"

Vasily smiled widely. "I like the cold. And anyway, this isn't *real* cold. At home, there's a layer of ice on the water troughs in the morning, more often than not."

Mother shuddered. "Sounds awful. I'm not much for the cold."

"Oh, Koroslova's not the place for you, then." Vasily nodded out at the horizon where glimpses of the ocean were just coming into view as they walked down the hill, the tops of the waves glistening under the night sky. "I miss the cold sometimes, but I do love this. All that water, as far as the eye can see. It makes me wish I could swim, but I never learned. It was far too cold. Besides, my father deemed it unseemly to be seen flailing around half-undressed in a pond."

"I'm the opposite. Spent my childhood messing about in boats. My dad was a fisherman." He gestured towards the ocean. "If you ever wanted to flail around half-undressed with someone, I'm your man."

He realised how that sounded just as Vasily let out a snort of laughter.

"Swimming! I meant swimming lessons!" he said hastily.

"Oh, I know," Vasily said, his teeth gleaming in the moonlight as he grinned, "and I'll keep your offer in mind."

"Well, mind you do," Mother said as they approached Rosie's. "When you live near the water, it makes sense to be able to keep yourself afloat."

They settled themselves at a table inside, out of the cold, and Rosie took their orders and brought them both a pint of pale ale. The place was busy as always, with two serving girls bustling between the tables without stopping. Mother nodded to one of the fishermen placing his order, and the man dipped his head in response.

Vasily looked around at the assortment of customers, most of them dock workers or fisherfolk, and looked at Mother, tilting his head. "If you don't mind me asking, if your father was a fisherman, why aren't you? How did you end up as a groom?"

Mother felt the familiar ache of loss in his chest, the one that never quite left no matter how much time had passed. He took a pull of ale to buy himself a moment as he considered how to reply. Finally, staring at the tabletop, he said, "I had an older brother. Drowned at twelve." His voice caught.

Vasily's sharp gasp was loud enough that it cut through the chatter of the café. "Oh gods. I'm so—"

"It happens," Mother said gruffly. "Perils of the sea and all that." He took another drink from his pint to ground himself, swallowing around the lump in his throat. It had been years and he'd only been a boy, but sometimes late at night, the sound of his mother sobbing at night still echoed in his mind. "My mum, she made me promise that I'd never work on the boats, and I wasn't going to say no to her, was I? I'd done some sweeping at the stables in town and found I was a dab hand with horses. So I went up to the castle once I was of age, got apprenticed as a groom, and I've never left."

He raised his head from the table to find Vasily staring at him, a look of horror in his face and his eyes wet. "That's—that's awful," he whispered. "I have three brothers, and I can't imagine losing one of them."

Mother was struck by an unfamiliar urge to reach across the table, run his thumb over Vasily's lashes, and gather the moisture clinging there. Instead, he said, "It was a long time ago, lad."

Vasily swallowed and scrubbed a hand across his eyes. "Of course. I'm sorry I asked."

"You weren't to know. And I could have told you to mind your beeswax." Mother did reach out then, patting Vasily's other hand where it rested on the table. "You're a good lad for caring."

"I'm soft, you mean," Vasily said with a watery smile.

"Nothing wrong with having a tender heart," Mother countered.

Vasily shrugged. "My father always said it was a sign of weakness. Maybe he's right."

"No, your father's a fool," Mother said, stung on Vasily's behalf. "It's not weak to have compassion. Just look at Mattias, the ex-chancellor. Prince Consort of Evergreen now, and before that he helped His Majesty run Lilleforth for years. He's smart as a whip, but that didn't stop him having a soft spot for helping people out of a difficult situation. I can't tell you how many people at the castle are grateful to him for hiring them, and every last one of them is bloody good at their jobs." His mouth quirked up in a smile. "He's the one who hired Felix, and that certainly worked out well for all concerned."

Vasily sat up straighter. "And he helped when my mother wrote to him, telling him I wanted to travel."

Mother was pleased to hear that Vasily had left home of his own free will, but he wondered once again who his family was that his mother was well enough acquainted with the chancellor that she was able to request favours.

"Well, it was a lucky day for me when he hired you." Mother patted Vasily's curled fingers once again. He was suddenly too aware of the warmth of Vasily's hand, the touch making his skin tingle.

Vasily ducked his head. "I think I was the lucky one."

Rosie arrived with their meals, and Vasily let out a moan of pleasure that was downright filthy as he bit into his first mouthful of cod and sauce. The sound caused heat to race through Mother, and his cock twitched in a way that brought back memories of the other night when he'd taken his pleasure. It was unexpected enough that it had him choking on his cider.

Vasily was out of his chair in seconds, patting him firmly on the back until Mother drew in a harsh breath. He ran his palms up and down Mother's spine in a soothing motion, and the touch of those warm, strong hands didn't do anything to diminish the heat coursing through Mother.

Even after Vasily took his hand away and sat back down, Mother could still feel the ghost of his touch like a brand on his skin, demanding Mother's attention—which was sheer foolishness. Vasily had been making sure he didn't choke, that was all. He didn't mean anything by it. And even if he had, Mother wasn't interested in people that way.

Or rather, he hadn't been. But maybe that had changed.

He closed his eyes and took a slow, deep breath as he tried to make sense of what he was feeling, and when he opened them, Vasily was watching him, his gaze filled with concern. "Mother?"

"I'm fine. Just catching my breath," he said, and shoved a forkful of cod into his mouth to prove just how fine he was while he came to grips with the fact that he was *definitely* attracted to someone.

No, not just someone.

Vasily.

Vasily, who was currently drinking his cider and had his head tipped back, exposing the long line of his throat in a way that was most distracting. Mother ducked his head and ate his meal, but he could have been eating boiled seaweed for all the attention he paid it.

While he chewed, he reminded himself that Vasily was in his employ and was more than ten years Mother's junior, and he was as green as the algae that grew on the rocks in the harbour. There was no way anything could happen between them.

And anyway, it was a moot point because Vasily clearly wasn't interested. He was busy trying to seduce *Jeremy*.

A lump settled in Mother's gut and he pushed his plate away, no longer hungry.

Vasily's forehead creased. "Is there something wrong with the cod?"

"Just tired," Mother lied, stretching his arms over his head in a fake yawn. Then, because Vasily was still watching him closely, he added, "Don't forget, I'm forty-two."

Vasily laughed, his entire face lighting up, and he was so pretty it made Mother's chest ache. But he forced a smile and laughed along with him, and Vasily didn't ask again if something was wrong, so Mother took it as a win.

When they left the café, Vasily hesitated at the end of the cobbled street. "Do you mind if we walk by the water for a bit? I know it's chilly, but I do love breathing in the salt. It's calming."

Mother was just about to say that he didn't mind at all when Vasily's eyes widened. "Oh gods. You probably don't want to go anywhere near the water, after your"—he swallowed—"your brother. Forget I said anything."

Mother's heart flip-flopped weirdly at Vasily's show of concern, and he was quick to reassure him. "Vasily," he said quietly, getting his attention. "If I didn't like the ocean, why would I come down to the docks for supper? I love it, lad. I've lived by the water my whole life, and you're right. It soothes the soul." He nodded at the nearby path, the one that didn't lead to the walled-in harbour but instead split off and went down to the beach. "Looks like the tide's out, so it should be nice for a walk."

Vasily's expression went from stricken to relieved in a heartbeat, and when Mother started walking down the path, Vasily was quick to follow, his boots crunching against the stones. They walked side by side down the path, which led them away from the fish markets and towards a sheltered bay with a long stretch of sandy shore.

Mother had spent many an hour paddling in the cool ocean water as a boy when the heat of summer had hit, and he smiled fondly at the memory of his mum, her skirts hitched up to her knees, holding his hand as he jumped over tiny waves and laughing when he fell on his arse even as she fished him out.

"What has you smiling?" Vasily asked.

"When I was a boy, Dad would be off on the boat, and Mum would bring us down to cool off of an afternoon. We always promised we wouldn't go past our knees, but somehow we always looked like drowned rats by the time she took us home. She never seemed to mind, though. It was probably easier than getting us to have a wash, now I think about it."

"Is she..." Vasily hesitated. "Is she still with you?"

"My mum? Aye, she's hale and hearty," Mother said as they walked at a leisurely pace along the beach, the moonlight reflecting off the water. "Dad, too. He's given up fishing, says he's too old for the early mornings, but he still takes the boat out. I think he'd be lost if he had to stay on dry land."

"I've never been on a boat. Not a real one, anyway. Only a rowboat once, in the little lake at the—at home." Vasily sounded wistful.

Mother wasn't sure why, but he found himself saying, "I could take you out if you wanted?"

Vasily turned to him, face alight with excitement. "Really?"

"I don't offer if I don't mean it, Vas."

"Vas," Vasily repeated, and his smile widened. "I've never had a nickname before."

"What, never?"

Vasily shook his head. "It's always been Vasily or Your—" He cut himself off. "Anyway, I like it."

"I do too," Mother said with a small smile. It felt special, having a name that was just theirs. "And I meant it about the boat. We can take my dad's skiff out."

"Oh, yes, please!" Vasily turned to him, beaming, and Mother felt a burst of affection that he was almost certain was caused by seeing Vasily smiling like that, just for him.

It was all very confusing.

Chapter Six

Vasily took a deep breath. It had been four days since Mother had suggested Vasily practice his romantic skills on him. He hadn't quite worked up the nerve yet, but he'd decided this morning that if he *did* wait until he'd gathered his nerve, his year would be over before he opened his mouth.

Besides, it was Mother, and Vasily found that he quite liked the idea of flirting with him, even if it was only pretend.

So now, having completed his tasks for the morning, he'd gone over to the main stable to seek Mother out and try his luck.

He found him crouched down examining the hooves of one the guard's horses. He squared his shoulders and stepped forward, all sorts of possible compliments floating around his brain. But when he opened his mouth, what came out was, "Your arse is magnificent in those trousers."

Mother tensed, his head whipping up, and he looked around, eyes wide and cheeks pink. "What?"

Vasily swallowed and took a step back, regretting this already. "I said, I like...you know what? Never mind."

Mother stood, knees cracking, and let go of the hoof he'd

been holding. It took a moment, but then the crease in Mother's brow cleared. "Wait. Was that you practicing your sweet talk?"

Vasily ran a hand down the side of his face. "It was me trying to, yes."

"And you thought that sneaking up on a man working with horse's hooves and telling him his arse looks good was the way to do it? Were you planning for me to get kicked in the head so you could nurse me back to health?" Mother huffed out a breath that wasn't quite a laugh, and the mare he was working with echoed it. He ran his hand down her flank, soothing her.

"I told you I'm bollocks at this." The tips of Vasily's ears burned as embarrassment raced through him.

Mother gave a wry smile. "You did mention my arse, so at least your intentions were clear. You're just lucky that neither Ginger nor I startle easily."

Vasily groaned. "It was too much, wasn't it?"

"Just a touch. Maybe next time try something simpler, like, 'You look fine today, Moth—Jeremy.'" Mother's lips pursed as if in disapproval.

Vasily nodded. "I was going for charming, but then I got distracted, and that's what came out of my mouth." He didn't feel the need to mention that it had been Mother's arse that had distracted him.

The corners of Mother's mouth twitched like he was suppressing a grin, and he reached out and ruffled Vasily's hair. "Ah, well. That's why we're practicing, right?"

"Right." Vasily's heart beat faster as he looked Mother up and down. His hair was tousled, as was the shirt he was wearing. It was a muted brown, but it caught the colour of his eyes in a way that was quite fetching. Vasily cleared his throat. "Can I... can I try again?"

Mother smiled, wide enough that small creases appeared at the corners of his eyes, evidence of a life spent living and working outdoors. "Of course, Vas. You have my full attention."

Vas.

His name sounded soft in Mother's mouth, and Vasily found he liked it there. He looked Mother over again, taking note of the arms folded over his chest and the corded muscle of his forearms. He thought briefly of commenting on those but decided to play it safe. "The, uh, the shirt you are wearing is very lovely."

Mother unfolded his arms and looked down at himself. "It's brown, lad."

"Yes, but it brings out the colour of your eyes. Which are also brown. And they're a nice brown, too. Like cocoa, not like horseshit. Which, now I think about it, is more green than brown."

Vasily cringed internally at the words, but Mother just shook his head and laughed. "You were doing so well there for a minute, lad. 'Your eyes are a nice brown, like cocoa' was a good start."

"I spoiled it with 'and not green like horseshit,' though, didn't I?"

"Just a touch. But admiring the shirt? That was good. If your man's not interested, you can both pass it off as an observation. And if he is, he can flutter his lashes and respond. Go on and try again," Mother said, nodding in encouragement. "Only try not mentioning shit this time."

"No shit, got it," he said, grinning. "Which, let's face it, is a good conversational guideline generally."

"Goes without saying, really." Mother folded his arms across his chest. "Have another go. Find something you like about me."

Vasily looked Mother up and down again, trying to decide. He wasn't handsome exactly, but he was attractive in a way that Vasily found hard to define. Maybe it was the laugh lines on his face that spoke of his good humour, or perhaps it was the leanly muscled physique gained as a result of hard work. Or it might have been his easy, open smile and the patience that shone in his deep brown eyes.

Whatever it was, Vasily found himself at a loss. How was he meant to choose just *one* thing he liked?

He might have gone on staring except Mother shuffled uncomfortably under his gaze, his arms dropping to his sides and something like hurt flitting across his features. "It's all right if you make something up," he said quietly. "It's not like this is real."

Vasily's heart clenched at the thought that Mother didn't think he had anything to offer. "No, it's not that," he said hastily. "It's that I'm spoilt for choice."

Mother raised an eyebrow, giving an uncertain smile, and Vasily pressed on. "My problem is that I can't choose just one thing. How can I, when there's so much to like about you?"

Mother's smile returned in full force, and Vasily found he could breathe a little easier. "Oh yes, lad. If you say things like that, you'll knock your young man off his feet."

"Thank you," Vasily said, right before he wondered why his gut twisted at the thought of saying those things to someone who wasn't Mother.

He patted Vasily on the shoulder. "We'll practice some more, and you'll be courting young Jeremy in no time. But for now, how about you help me check the rest of these hooves?"

"Of course," Vasily said, basking in the warmth of the smile Mother gave him. They moved through the rest of the stable, working side by side in companionable silence even as Mother's words rang in Vasily's ears and his mind whirled. Because while he was pleased that he'd successfully flirted, Vasily found to his surprise that Jeremy wasn't the person who came to mind when he imagined using his new skills for real.

Rather, it was a certain stablemaster with long legs, a crooked smile, and laughing brown eyes.

THE STABLEMASTER'S HEART

~

Vasily spent that night lying in bed thinking of other things to say to Mother that might pass as romantic, more encouraged by his eventual success this afternoon than he'd thought he'd be. It was gratifying in a way he hadn't expected, to have someone respond to his overtures—even if it *was* only make-believe.

Mindful of Mother's comment about avoiding flying hooves, he waited to try again until they were walking up to the castle for supper. "Nice night tonight," he said casually, glancing up at the clear skies and full moon. "Cold, though."

"Mmm," Mother said, his hands tucked under his armpits. "Bloody cold."

Vasily swallowed. "I could warm you up a bit if you like?" He extended a hand, palm open, like he expected Mother to take him up on his offer—not that he really thought he *would*, but if he was going to try this, he was going to do it right.

Mother stopped walking for a moment and looked at him, head tilted, before smiling. "I'd appreciate that," he said, lacing their fingers together. The coolness of his touch was offset by the warm glow that spread through Vasily from head to toe.

He expected Mother to let go of him after a few steps, but he kept their hands linked until they were almost at the castle, shortening his long strides so that they were side by side. He gave Vasily's hand a squeeze and only let go as they approached the side gate. "Well done, Vas."

"Thank you." Vasily ducked his head to hide the heat that rose in his cheeks at the compliment.

He couldn't hold back his grin, though, and he found himself smiling all through dinner and laughing with Ollie over the newest stable boy's misadventures in sorting out the tack. The poor lad had managed to get the reins tied in a knot around his ankle, of all places. It reminded him of the conversation he'd had with Mother, and Vasily reflected that he'd been right—with some more practice, surely he'd be able to gather up the nerve to talk to Jeremy and make his interest known.

As if summoned by a thought, Jeremy slotted into place across from him at the trestle table. "Vasily, my foreign prince!" he exclaimed, arms spread wide.

He froze, all the blood draining from his face. "What did you call me?"

Jeremy grinned. "My prince among men. My treasure from a foreign land."

Vasily stared at him blankly, trying to make sense of his words and wondering who'd revealed his secret, and Jeremy's smile faded.

"It was, I was just..." Jeremy ran a hand down the back of his neck, ducking his head. "Forget it."

Vasily stared a moment longer before understanding flooded through him and he laughed, mainly from relief. "*Oh!* It was a term of affection."

Next to him, Mother scowled and muttered, "Could have fooled me." Louder, he said, "I don't need any more princes in my stables, *thank you very much.*" Then he fixed Jeremy with a glare that had him picking up his plate and scurrying away to the other end of the table.

Vasily felt like he'd missed something important, but his attention was taken up by Mother's comment. "What princes have you had in your stables?"

Mother grinned, and it suited him much better than the scowl he'd been wearing a minute ago. "Well, do you mean the one who's a prince now because he married the king, or the other one?"

"There was *another one?*"

Mother nodded, taking the time to finish his mouthful of pottage before he spoke. "Aye. Prince Davin worked as a stable boy. Well," he said, eyes sparkling with amusement, "I *say* worked. But he was fair useless for a good long while. Spent all his time skiving off to spoon the maids."

Vasily's brow furrowed. He'd heard odds and ends about King Leopold's heir from the wrong side of the sheets, but he hadn't known he'd worked for Mother. "Why, though?"

Mother raised his eyebrows. "Why was he spooning the maids? Because he's his father's son, lad."

"No, why was he a stable hand?"

"Oh! That was because, according to his mother, he was turning into an entitled little tit, so she sent him to be taken in hand. The chancellor decided the stables was as good a place as any for him to learn the value of a solid day's work." Mother grinned widely. "He got there in the end, though. Turns out, finding out he was heir to the throne was the kick up the arse he needed, and he wasn't useless after all."

"You'd think it would go the other way, though," Ollie said from where he was sitting on Vasily's other side. "If I found out I was a prince, you wouldn't catch me shovelling shit. I'd be spending my days reclining on a couch and having someone bring me trays of cakes."

"I don't think that's how being a prince works," Vasily said, fighting the urge to tell Ollie about the hours of lessons in etiquette and languages and diplomacy he'd sat through.

"Aye," Mother chimed in. "You wouldn't catch me getting involved with royalty."

Vasily ducked his head and concentrated on his food, trying to ignore the sinking feeling in his gut. Even if he hadn't been a prince, Mother wouldn't be interested in him.

And Vasily wasn't interested in Mother that way either. He was interested in *Jeremy*.

Wasn't he?

He chewed and swallowed mindlessly, the conversation flowing around him, and as he ate, it dawned on him that he didn't actually care all that much about Jeremy. He looked very fine in his uniform, to be sure, and he had a handsome enough countenance and was pleasant to talk to, but there was nothing that made him special and nothing that inclined Vasily to court him—except for the fact that he'd indicated he found Vasily appealing.

Mother, though? He was *intriguing*.

Vasily was drawn from his thoughts by Mother standing and taking his bowl. His dinner was gone, but he didn't remember eating it. "I'll bring you back some pudding, lad," Mother said, and then he was gone, walking over to the serving table before Vasily could blink.

He came back with two servings of custard, and Vasily got a swooping sensation in his stomach. Mother was taking care of him—and he wasn't doing it because Vasily was a prince but because he wanted to.

Because he *liked* Vasily.

Mother sat across from him and slid the bowl his way, and Vasily took it with a smile of thanks and started eating. The custard was delicious and was gone far too soon. Vasily licked his lips to catch the last traces of sweetness there, and when he glanced up, it was to find Mother staring at him, his own custard untouched and his gaze fixed on Vasily's mouth for some reason. He licked his lips again reflexively, and Mother's Adam's apple bobbed as he swallowed.

Vasily nodded at his full plate. "Not hungry?"

Mother cleared his throat. "Aye," he said gruffly, ducking his head as he ate, the tops of his ears pink.

Vasily glanced around to find that the others at the table had gone, leaving them alone. It was the perfect opportunity to practice his wooing skills. His fingertips drummed against the wooden surface of the table as he tried to think of something to say. It was all very well Mother promising to make a smooth talker of him, but he wasn't there yet. Still, he wasn't going to get any better if he didn't try, was he?

"I, um. The custard was delicious."

Mother glanced up.

Vasily, heart hammering against his ribs for reasons he couldn't quite define, leaned forward so their heads were barely an inch apart and, in what he hoped was a sultry manner, said, "Of course, the custard isn't the only delicious thing around here."

Mother's brow creased. "Did you want some of the cake? I can fetch you a slice if you want."

"No, Mother." Vasily huffed in frustration. Why was this so difficult? He let his head drop to the table with a thunk and mumbled, "I meant *you*."

Mother sputtered around his spoon. "*Me*?"

Vasily flapped a hand, his head still resting on the table. "Never mind. I'll never be good at this."

Mother put his spoon down. "Vasily." A firm hand gripped his chin, gently guiding him upright. Mother gazed at him, brown eyes wide and sincere. "You surprised me, that's all. But if you *were* wooing me and you said that, we'd be halfway back to the cottage by now."

Vasily brightened at that. "Really?"

"Really." Mother ran a hand down the back of his neck, ducking his head. "You keep that up and you'll enchant your young man." Something like unhappiness flitted across his features, there and gone again like a cloud passing over the sun. Then he smiled, a weak, uncertain thing, and pushed his uneaten custard to one side. "Shall we go back?"

Mother remained quiet as they started the walk back, and Vasily was just wondering if he'd upset him somehow when fingertips grazed his, and he glanced down to see Mother extending a hand. "Warm me up?" he said, his smile more genuine this time.

He slid his palm into Mother's, giving a squeeze, and Mother leaned in close, their shoulders bumping together as they ambled along the path. They seemed to be walking far more slowly than normal, and Vasily couldn't help but be glad of it because it meant he got to enjoy Mother's touch, as innocent as it was, for a little longer.

Eventually, though, they reached the door of Mother's cottage, their breath coming out in frosty white plumes. Vasily knew that a chilly evening was no time to be dallying on doorsteps, but he couldn't seem to bring himself to let go of Mother's hand. They stood there in the cold evening air, close enough that Mother's face was mere inches from his, his lips parted as he gazed down, and Vasily realised that he wasn't the only one making no move to untangle their fingers.

He thought back over the evening. About how Mother had reacted to Jeremy. About how *he'd* reacted to Jeremy. About how nervous he'd been when trying to compliment Mother—almost like he'd meant it.

Because you did.

When Vasily's mother had read him fairy tales as a boy, he'd always imagined a happy ending—and a handsome prince—for himself. Mother Jones was not a conventionally handsome man, and he was certainly no prince, but still, Vasily felt the same stirring ache in his chest now that he had when he was a little boy imagining his happy ending. He looked down at their clasped hands and awareness rolled over him, like an ocean wave breaking on the shores of his attraction, and he wondered how he'd been so blind.

He didn't want to flirt with Jeremy. He wanted to flirt with Mother.

He wanted to *kiss* Mother.

And maybe, if the way he was standing close was any indication, Mother wanted to kiss him too. He recalled how Mother had snapped at Jeremy over nothing—like a dog guarding a bone—or, if he thought about it, like a jealous lover.

Surely not, he chided himself. But still, a thrill ran through him at the thought of Mother wanting him.

He must have stood there too long because Mother cleared his throat. "I suppose I'd best—"

"Wait!"

Mother stopped mid-sentence, and Vasily tilted his head back so he could gaze into those deep brown eyes. And perhaps he was imagining it, but he could have sworn what he saw reflected there was his own longing.

For a moment all his years of hiding who and what he was threatened to overwhelm him, and he almost stepped away—almost—but then the corners of Mother's mouth curved up in a smile, and Vasily *wanted*.

He reminded himself that he was a *prince*, and if there was one thing he'd been trained to do, it was to stand straight, speak clearly, and say what he wanted without hesitation.

So he did.

"Mother Jones," he said, ignoring the slight tremor in his voice, "I should very much like to kiss you."

Chapter Seven

Mother's breath caught in his throat, and his stomach clenched around the rock that had formed there. He reminded himself that Vasily didn't mean what he'd said—no matter how much Mother wanted him to.

Because Vasily wanted *Jeremy*, and this was just him practicing.

It was hard to remember that, though, when Vasily had held his hand and laughed over dinner with him. And it didn't help that Vasily had ignored Jeremy's clumsy advances—had seemed almost distressed by them, in fact. It had made jealousy flare hot and strong in Mother's chest, and he hadn't been able to help scowling until the boy had taken the hint and left.

Afterwards, Mother had felt slightly guilty because wasn't he meant to be *helping* Vasily win Jeremy's affections? But the guilt had faded when Vasily hadn't given Jeremy a second look all evening, and Mother had hoped that meant Vasily had realized the boy wasn't right for him.

Except here he was, practicing asking for kisses, and it was taking all of Mother's strength not to take Vasily at his word, because for the first time in his life, he wanted that too—to taste

Vasily's mouth and run his hands down his spine, to feel smooth skin under his palms and...well. It didn't matter what else he wanted, because he wasn't going to get it, was he?

Vasily was still waiting for an answer, eyes wide and expectant, and Mother knew what he wanted to hear. "If you ask Jeremy like that, he'll kiss you for certain." The words tasted like ash in his mouth.

Vasily blinked and then shook his head rapidly. "No, I—" He reached out his free hand and cupped Mother's cheek. "I wasn't planning on asking Jeremy. I'm asking *you*, Mother. You're the one I want to kiss." He moved closer, near enough that their breath mingled, then tilted his head back, lips parted in invitation.

Mother's heart stuttered in his chest and something like a breathless laugh escaped him. "Me?" he asked, his stomach swooping as his emotions veered between hope and disbelief.

"You." Vasily's eyes shone with anticipation. "Will you kiss me?"

His heart soared.

Vasily wanted him.

Mother didn't have much experience, but it seemed as natural as breathing to cup the back of Vasily's head in one palm and hold him in place. He leant forward that last fraction of an inch, eyes closing as he did so, and pressed their lips together in a chaste kiss.

Vasily's mouth was soft and he tasted of custard, and it took Mother's breath away. He pulled away after a few seconds, his lips tingling, and Vasily grinned widely. Then, with none of the shyness Mother might have expected, Vasily clutched at his shoulders, pulled him close and kissed him again, more firmly this time. His tongue pressed, clumsy but persistent, against the seam of Mother's mouth, and he yielded to the pressure.

Vasily licked his way inside, teasing, exploring, their tongues brushing together—and *how*, exactly, was the act of pressing two mouths together this good? It made no sense, but one kiss from Vasily and suddenly there was a fire burning low in Mother's belly, heat in his veins, and a desperate need for more.

Mother put everything he had into the kiss. Something like lightning raced through him when he slid his hand down Vasily's spine just like he'd imagined, moving so they were pressed against each other, making Vasily moan into his mouth.

They kissed until Mother had to pull back, his breath coming in short gasps. In all honesty he wanted nothing more than to keep doing what they were doing, but his cock was hardening in his trousers with an unaccustomed urgency. If Vasily kept making noises like that and touching him the way he was, Mother wasn't sure he'd be able to stop what they'd started—and Vasily *had* only asked for a kiss.

Vasily's eyes were dark pools, the pupils blown wide, and his cheeks were flushed. He let out a shaky breath. "I, um. That was. Yes." He laughed, high and breathless, and leaned back against the door.

"It was," Mother agreed, voice cracking. He clenched his hands against his sides to fight off the temptation to drag Vasily in and taste him again.

Even *thinking* about kissing Vasily had his cock throbbing against his lacings.

Vasily stood there biting his lip, one hand cupping the obvious bulge in the front of his trousers. He stepped forward, draping his arms around Mother's neck, and then he was kissing Mother again, gentle and soft and careful like he was something precious.

The rasp of Vasily's unshaven skin against Mother's cheek had his heart racing and his blood heating, and he suddenly understood all those times he'd come across Felix and his king in the stables with their shirts untucked and their faces flushed.

If kissing someone you cared for felt like this, how was anybody meant to resist it? And if this was what kissing was like, what would it feel like to get Vasily *naked,* to run his fingers through that thatch of blond chest hair and trace the muscled lines of his back?

His cock bucked against his lacings, and Mother wrenched back, panting, before he ended up spilling in his trousers. Vasily's brow creased. "What is it?"

He shook his head, holding up one finger, and when he trusted himself to speak, he said, "It was only meant to be a kiss, Vas."

Vasily looked pointedly down at the obvious bulge in the front of his own trousers. "What if I want more?" he asked, one eyebrow raised.

Mother's heart raced and his cock firmed at the prospect. "More?"

"*More,*" Vasily said. His tone was firm even though he was blushing to the roots of his hair, and Mother wanted *so* badly to say yes.

But underneath the sheer overwhelming want he felt right now, there was one simple truth that rang out. Vasily was something special. Mother desired him, yes, but he wanted more than doorstep kisses and one night. So he closed his eyes and took several slow, deep breaths until he had himself under some semblance of control.

He opened his eyes to find Vasily staring at him, wearing a hurt expression that made his heart clench. "It's not that I don't want you, lad," he said, his voice rough. "I want you more than I've ever wanted anyone. But I don't do"—he waved a hand up and down Vasily's body— "this. Well, I *didn't,*" he said, "but you have me feeling things, *wanting* things, that I never have. And I don't want to rush."

Vasily's expression cleared. "So, this isn't you saying no?"

Mother hesitated before deciding that if he was telling the truth, he might as well tell the whole truth. "I don't want a quick fumble in a doorway, Vasily. I want this to *be* something. I want to—" He cleared his throat. "I want to court you," he said firmly.

The lad's face broke into a wide smile. "I want that too."

Mother's heart raced the way it did when he was on horseback, exhilaration washing over him. "Then we'll do that."

Vasily licked his lips. "With kissing? And all the rest of it?"

"With kissing, and all the rest of it, in time," Mother agreed, smiling so hard his face hurt. "Whatever you'd like."

Vasily stepped forward and tipped Mother's head to the side, nuzzling at the tender skin there and sending a thrill running through him that made his cock throb with renewed interest. He cupped Mother's face in one hand, his eyes wide. "Is...was that all right?"

"It was bloody marvellous," Mother rasped out, right before he tangled his fingers in Vasily's long hair and kissed him again, a messy clash of teeth and tongues that was more enthusiasm than style but somehow still managed to be the better than it had any right to be.

Vasily moaned into his mouth, and Mother took a moment to preen over his stunned expression when he pulled back. Then he forced himself to say, "I think you'd better go before we get carried away."

Vasily blinked slowly, like he was coming back from somewhere far away. "Right. Yes. Going slow."

Mother nodded.

Sighing, Vasily said, "Then I'll see you for breakfast." He leaned in and pressed a kiss to Mother's cheek before flashing him a bright smile, then turning and half stumbling down the path slightly hunched over.

Mother watched him for a second before yanking the door of the cottage open and stepping inside. He groaned and threw himself into the chair by the fire, his cock a hard, persistent ache that demanded to be dealt with.

Gods, how was he expected to think when he was consumed with want like this?

He squirmed uncomfortably, and his hand crept to the lacings of his trousers. Almost without thinking, he found himself loosening the fastenings and shoving his hand inside, taking himself in hand and sighing with relief as he stroked his cock.

Mother closed his eyes and ran his tongue over his bottom lip, chasing the traces of Vasily's kisses, and imagined it was Vasily touching him. He groaned as another bolt of unaccustomed lust shot through him, his cock leaking.

He bit his lip, tensing, and rubbed a thumb over his cockhead, spreading the slick there. His heart thundered in his chest and his balls drew up tight. He was so close, just a tug was all he—

There was a knock at the door, and he yanked his hand away and sat upright, breathing fast.

"Mother?"

Vasily.

Mother stood and tried to stuff himself back into his trousers, and when that didn't quite work, he left his shirt untucked, hoping it would cover the evidence of his arousal. He yanked the door open to find Vasily standing there, eyes bright. His hair had come free from its usual leather tie and was falling around his face in loose waves, his cheeks were flushed, and his chest was heaving like he'd run to get there. He didn't wait for an invitation but stepped inside and cupped Mother's face in one hand. "I know we said we'd go slow, but I don't want slow. I want *you.*"

And what was Mother supposed to say to that, when his own need was just as great? Still, he forced himself to ask. "Are you sure? It's fine if you want to wait."

Vasily tilted his head and then, with a gleam in his eye, draped his arms over Mother's shoulders and said, "I've waited to be with an attractive man my entire life. I don't want to wait any longer."

Then Vasily kissed him, hot and hungry, and all thoughts of taking their time vanished. Vasily moaned and Mother's arousal bloomed fresh, although it was tinged with nerves. What, exactly, did Vasily want from him? And what if he expected Mother to have experience at this kind of thing?

But his nervousness didn't have a chance to take hold before Vasily was kissing him again, more gently this time. Mother lost himself in the softness of his lips, the silkiness of his hair, the heat of another man's body against his own. His blood raced hot through his veins. Vasily reached down and tugged at the lacings on Mother's shirt, and he made an appreciative sound as his fingers traced over Mother's exposed collarbones.

"Mother—" He bit his lip.

"Hmmm?"

"It's—don't laugh, and please, for the love of the gods, don't be offended, but does anyone ever call you anything else? Because I don't think I can call you Mother when I'm asking for your cock in my mouth."

Mother drew in a sharp breath, not at the comment about his name—he was used to those—but at the image of Vasily on his knees, his full mouth wrapped around Mother's length. All the blood in his body rushed south, his cock filling until he was so hard it *ached*.

"Bryn," he managed to get out. "Call me Bryn." It was the name he was meant to have had, the one he didn't share, but it seemed right to share it with Vasily.

"Bryn," Vasily said slowly, tasting the name, and then his smile was back, and he leaned in and pressed a kiss to Mother's cheek. "My Bryn."

It shouldn't have been arousing, but something about hearing his secret name in Vasily's lilting accent sent a shiver of want racing through his veins.

Or perhaps it wasn't the name. Perhaps it was the *my*.

Whichever it was, Mother liked it. He tipped his head and caught Vasily's mouth with his and they shared another long, lingering kiss. When Vasily slid both hands down Mother's back and cupped his arse, pulling their bodies tight, the closeness and the press of warm muscle against him had the heat in his belly flaring and becoming more urgent. He surged forward and backed Vasily against the closed door, rocking his hips forward and chasing more contact until Vasily let out a broken whimper.

Mother tensed and stilled. Had he been too forward? Was it too much? Vasily had *said*—

"Do that again, Bryn," Vasily gasped, tilting his head back and grasping Mother's arse tighter.

Well, that answered that question.

Vasily was beautiful like this, with his head back and his lips parted, and Mother gave in to the temptation to lean in and place a line of kisses down Vasily's throat, the skin soft under his lips. Vasily shuddered under the touch, letting out a broken moan, and the sound was so desperate, so wanton, that it almost had Mother spilling in his trousers right there.

He buried his face in the curve of Vasily's throat, taking slow, deep breaths. Vasily slid one hand up the back of Mother's shirt, his fingertips leaving warm trails where they traced over his skin, the other hand stilling when it found the opened lacing of Mother's trousers and his obvious erection. "Bryn, can I?"

Mother wasn't sure what he was asking exactly, but it didn't matter. He wanted anything and everything Vasily would give him. He reached down and pulled the front of his trousers open farther in a wordless response.

Vasily slid his hand inside, fumbling as he wrapped it around Mother's length and engulfed it, the touch like a brand against his skin. "Oh! It's different when it's someone else," Vasily said, breathless. He slid his hand up and down, his movements hesitant, and Mother thought his heart might beat right out of his chest.

Then Vasily slid his hand over the head of Mother's cock, capturing the moisture that was gathering there and spreading the slickness over his palm. Mother groaned, and Vasily licked his lips and nodded to himself before taking hold once again with more certainty and pumping Mother's cock in a steady rhythm.

"*Gods above*," Mother rasped, his entire world narrowing down to the heat of Vasily's touch, the slick slide of his hand, and the tightening of Mother's balls as pleasure threatened to overwhelm him.

Vasily sped up his movements, and when he skated his thumb back and forth over Mother's leaking slit. It was too much and just right all at once. Mother doubled over, groaning like he'd been punched when his climax hit him. Vasily made a wounded noise of his own but Mother barely noticed, too caught up in his world exploding as he forgot how to breathe and, just for the briefest moment, his vision whited out.

Mother rocked and panted through his climax with Vasily's hand still loosely cupped around his softening cock. Afterwards, when Mother could stand straight, Vasily tucked his head in the crook of his neck and let out a satisfied hum, his breath warm against Mother's skin. "Gods, Bryn," he said breathlessly. When he lifted his head, his pupils were blown wide, his gaze glassy.

Mother was still lightheaded from the strength of his orgasm, but he'd been brought up to be considerate, so he said, "What about you, Vas? Do you want me to—"

"No need," Vasily said, his cheeks darkening. "I already, um."

He shuffled awkwardly, glancing down between them, and when Mother followed his gaze, he saw a damp patch on Vasily's trousers. "Oh. *Oh.*"

"I told you I didn't want slow," Vasily said. He wiped his messy hand on the untucked tail of his shirt, and his mouth quirked up into a bashful grin. "Watching you lose control, it was...you were breathtaking, and I couldn't help myself."

Mother felt something like pride swell in his chest. He'd never had that effect on anyone before, and he found he liked it. He smiled, reaching out to tuck a stray lock of hair behind Vasily's ear. "Next time, I'll make sure I get my hands on you first."

Vasily's breath caught. "Next time?"

Mother leaned in and stole a brief kiss. "Next time. After all, we *are* courting, aren't we?"

Vasily's answering smile was like a sunrise, and Mother could have basked in the warmth of it all day.

They stood like that, leaning into each other while they recovered. Mother never wanted the moment to end, but he was uncomfortably aware of his soft cock hanging out of his trousers, and so with a sigh he stood up straight and tucked himself away.

Vasily bit his lip. "I should go."

But he made no move to leave, and Mother found himself saying, "Would you like to stay?"

Vasily gave a small, pleased smile. "Really?"

"Really," Mother said, his world still warm and pleasantly fuzzy round the edges.

"Then yes, please," Vasily said, wrapping his arms around Mother and nuzzling his throat. "If I wake up in the night, I want you right there next to me so I can be sure this is real and not just some glorious dream."

Mother smiled to himself and pressed a kiss to Vasily's temple.

He felt exactly the same way.

Chapter Eight

Vasily stirred the pot over the hearth with intense concentration, careful to keep the porridge from sticking to the bottom. A loud snort made him jump and the spoon clattered, but when he looked over at the bed, Mother—*Bryn*—slept on. Vasily couldn't keep the smile off his face as he recalled the night before.

There had been a certain awkwardness to getting ready for bed because even though he'd held Mother's cock in his hand and made him come—and hadn't *that* made him feel like a minor god?—it was still a big step, being naked in front of another man. But Vasily had summoned all his courage and shrugged his way out of his messy trousers and underthings, and the way Mother had gazed at him with his mouth slightly open and his eyes dark, like Vasily was *desirable*, had chased away any remaining shyness.

Then Mother had pushed his own clothing off, and Vasily had been too busy ogling to care about his own nudity, because Mother's body was nothing short of glorious. His long frame was adorned with a surprising amount of lean muscle and dark chest hair, and he sported a very pretty cock. Mother had raised an eyebrow at Vasily's silent admiration. "Pass muster, does it?"

"You're gorgeous, Bryn," Vasily had said quietly, and he'd meant it.

Mother had made a pleased chuffing noise that had reminded Vasily of the horses when they were given a treat. "So I don't need to find a nightshirt then?"

He'd shaken his head vigorously and Mother had laughed. When they'd crawled into bed together under a well-worn quilt that still bore faint traces of its original blues and greens, they'd spent some time kissing and running their hands over each other. It hadn't gone further, though, both of them happy for now with just getting to touch, and it had been as easy as breathing to let himself be turned on his side as Mother spooned him from behind.

Vasily didn't remember falling asleep, but he'd woken to find himself encircled in strong arms, and he'd lain there enjoying the unfamiliar sensation of another man's body next to his. Then Mother had shifted and his erection had pressed into Vasily's arse, and Vasily wasn't *quite* there yet—except in his fantasies—so he'd slipped out of bed. After wrinkling his nose at his cum-stained clothing, he'd reluctantly put the trousers on and crept out into the predawn light and back to his own cottage, where he'd washed and changed into something less...crackly, before ducking back down the path to Mother's and starting breakfast.

Vasily dragged the spoon through the porridge and was pleased to find that there were none of the customary lumps. He lifted the pot off the hob and set it to one side, then set the water to boil for their morning tea.

"Something smells good," Mother said from the depths of the quilt, voice raspy with sleep.

"I made porridge, and it isn't even lumpy!" Vasily moved over to the corner of the room where Mother's bed was and, feeling bold, lay down on top of the faded quilt next to him.

Mother rolled towards him and blinked owlishly, and for a moment Vasily worried that he was regretting last night, but then he gave a sleepy half smile. Combined with his messy hair and stubble, it was so charming that Vasily couldn't help but lean over and kiss him. Mother gave a contented hum when they parted and sat up, and Vasily got to see the muscles in his shoulders flex temptingly when he stretched his arms over his head and yawned. He still couldn't quite believe that Mother had asked to court him. It was something he hadn't known he could have, but as soon as Mother had offered, it had felt right. He couldn't stop smiling, his stomach fluttering with excitement and nerves both.

Mother pressed a kiss to Vasily's cheek, his stubble scraping against his skin and sending a shiver up Vasily's spine. "Glad to see you haven't run screaming. I woke earlier and you were gone."

He ran his fingers through the bird's nest of Mother's hair, untangling it. "I just went to get something to wear. I didn't want to wake you."

"Aye, I slept solid last night. Must have been the company." He gave his crooked smile and Vasily blushed, remembering the press of Mother's erection against his arse. He certainly *had* slept solid.

The water on the hearth bubbled and roiled, stray droplets making angry hissing sounds as they came in contact with the pot, and Vasily shook his head to clear away his musings about Mother's cock. He cleared his throat. "Anyway, breakfast's ready." He slipped off the bed and busied himself making the tea while Mother dressed and ducked outside to the privy, and by the time Mother had washed his face and worked his hair into some semblance of order, the porridge was in two bowls on the table along with steaming mugs of tea.

Mother sat and took a bite, and his face lit up with pleasure. "Good job, lad. We'll make a cook out of you yet."

Warmth flooded Vasily's chest at the praise, and he grinned around his own spoon. The porridge wasn't perfect, but it was a far cry from the inedible messes he'd produced the first few times he'd tried. Being able to feed oneself was a silly thing to be proud of, he supposed, especially for a prince, but there it was.

He tried very hard not to think about the fact he was going to have to *tell* Mother he was a prince at some stage. Surely it wouldn't matter.

Would it?

They ate quietly but it wasn't awkward, more both of them gathering their thoughts. When the bowls were empty, Mother took them to wipe clean, and it was while his back was turned that Mother said, "So, no regrets about last night?"

There was a note of uncertainty in his tone.

Vasily didn't hesitate, pushing his chair back and walking over to wrap his arms around Mother's waist from behind, resting his head against his back. "None. My only regret is that I didn't see what was in front of me sooner." Vasily pressed his lips to the nape of Mother's neck, and the tense set of his shoulders loosened under the touch.

Vasily wondered if he was terrible for wanting to drag Mother back to bed and indulge in some more of that touching he'd enjoyed so much last night, perhaps even taking things further. Not *too* much further, not yet, but he'd often wondered what it would be like to get his mouth on another man's cock, and Mother had seemed to like the idea last night.

Before he had a chance to suggest anything, though, Mother turned in his grasp and draped his arms around Vasily's neck. "We should go and see to the horses." Vasily only had a moment to be disappointed before he added, "Earlier we start, earlier we're done, and we might have time for some more"— Mother swallowed, and the tips of his ears turned pink— "canoodling."

Vasily's heart fluttered, and he pressed a kiss to Mother's

forehead, standing on his tiptoes to reach. "I like canoodling with you, Bryn."

Mother grinned. "Same, lad." He slid his palm down Vasily's spine, leaving a warm trail in its wake before withdrawing his hand with a small sigh. "Horses first, though. We're in the service of the king, remember."

"Yes, right. Horses first. Canoodling later," Vasily agreed before stealing a kiss.

Once Mother had pulled his boots on, they walked across to the stables. Ollie and their newest stable boy, Conor, were already hard at work filling the feed troughs and Mother nodded in satisfaction. He walked the length of the stalls, inspecting the horses for any sign of illness or upset, but they all appeared clear-eyed and content.

He and Vasily helped distribute the feed, and once the horses had eaten, they set about releasing them into the adjoining grazing meadows. That was the cue for the stable boys to set to work mucking out the stalls, and after making sure they were getting into all the corners, Mother walked with Vasily over to where Shadow and Blackbird were kept.

Vasily fed Blackbird half a carrot while Mother did the same for Shadow, stroking his broad nose and murmuring nonsense, his forearms flexing enticingly as he moved. Vasily licked his lips and reminded himself they had a job to do and now was *not* the time to be looking at Mother's arms. Or his arse. Or his long legs that held a very pretty cock between them, one that Vasily wanted to see more of.

It didn't take long to get the horses fed and turned out, and Vasily grabbed a shovel and started cleaning out Blackbird's stall, scooping up the muck and carrying it to the pile outside. Mother worked alongside him, and soon enough both stalls were fresh and clean. When they were finished, Mother wiped the back of his hand across his forehead, the skin of his throat glistening with the light sweat he'd worked up. He stood there, his shirt clinging to him, and Vasily found himself drawn like a moth to a flame. Before he knew it, he was standing right in front of him, one hand settling on Mother's waist as he leaned in for a kiss.

Mother stilled for a split second but then his hands were at Vasily's hips, and he was kissing him back. The pleased little sounds he was making between the soft brushes of their lips left Vasily in no doubt that he was enjoying himself.

Vasily found himself backed against the door to Blackbird's stall, Mother's hand cupping the back of his head and angling it just right as he licked against the seam of Vasily's mouth. Vasily opened to his touch, and the taste of him was already familiar, like they'd been doing this forever. He let out a contented noise of his own, tangling his hands in Mother's hair and ignoring the way the timbers of the stall door dug into his hip, concentrating instead on the scrape of Mother's ever-present stubble against his skin and the warmth of his touch. He pulled Mother closer and they kissed, slow and lazy. There was no real heat to it, but it was still thrilling in its own way, because was anything better than stealing kisses from the man he was courting?

Vasily didn't think so.

They drew back at the same time and Vasily ran a fingertip over his mouth, lips tingling, and sighed.

"I know, lad," Mother said with a rueful grin, "but we should save it for later. Last thing we need is Ollie barrelling in here and then telling the world and its wife what we're about."

It shouldn't have stung like it did. Still, something in Vasily's chest ached, sharp and unexpected, at the implication that what they were doing was something shameful, something to be hidden. It cut too close to the bone, an unwelcome reminder of home.

Disappointment and loss flooded through him. "So you want to court me, but only in secret? Are you ashamed to be with a"—his voice cracked—"a man?"

Mother's brow creased. "Of course not."

"Then why do you care if anyone sees?" Vasily forced the words out. He'd foolishly thought Mother actually wanted to court him, but he should have known better.

He was a dalliance, nothing more.

As he stepped back, Mother followed, placing one hand on his forearm. Vasily desperately wanted to pull away, but Mother's touch was far more comforting than it had a right to be. His brow was creased, but his voice was soft when he said, "I'm *proud* to be courting you, Vasily Petrov. But I won't have it bandied about as gossip." He snorted. "*Ashamed*, my eye. The truth of it is I can't wait to walk up to the castle with you on my arm and show you off as mine."

The band around Vasily's chest loosened and he found himself able to breathe again. "Really?"

"Really. Look at you. You're young, charming, and gorgeous to boot. Why *wouldn't* I be proud to be seen with you? But there's protocol to consider. You *work* for me, Vasily. It's only proper that I let His Majesty and His Highness know that we're courting and get their approval before they hear it from their valet or one of the guards."

Vasily had to admit that the desire to follow protocol was understandable, especially for a man like Mother, who was as proper as they came when royalty was involved. He wondered fleetingly what Mother would say when he found out about Vasily's heritage and shoved the thought aside to deal with later.

"I suppose that makes sense." He placed his hand over Mother's where it still rested on his forearm and rubbed slow circles on the back of his hand with his thumb. "And now I understand your reasons, I'm happy to be discreet until you've spoken to them—although surely those two would be the *last* ones to object to a romance between their grooms."

Mother gave a wry smile. "Aye, well. There's one rule for the rich and another for the rest of us. Not that I begrudge them their happiness," he hastened to add. "Lord knows King Leopold deserves someone in his corner with the job he has running the kingdom, and I've always liked Felix. But I imagine it's a different world when you're a prince, isn't it?"

"I imagine it is," Vasily said, thinking about the stifling luxury of the palace he'd grown up in and the obligations he'd avoided by hanging around the stables.

"I was thinking I might talk to His Majesty and His Highness today," Mother said, pulling him out of his thoughts. He leaned in and pressed a kiss to Vasily's lips, gentle and reassuring, and Vasily kissed him back.

"Talk to us about wha—oh!" Prince Felix said, striding into the stables and stopping short.

"Why are you standing in the doorway, Flick—*ohhhh,*" said King Leopold, coming to a halt next to his husband.

Vasily pulled back, his face burning. "Sires," he said, addressing them both as he ran a hand over his mouth, mortification washing over him. He'd never been caught kissing anyone before, and he wondered if they'd get in trouble.

Felix tilted his head, regarding Vasily steadily. Unable to take the silence, Vasily blurted out, "I'm sorry about kissing in the stables!"

Mother snorted, and to Vasily's surprise he didn't seem the least bit taken aback. "Trust me, these two have done much worse in here."

"That was one time!" Felix said.

Mother raised an eyebrow, and Leopold elbowed Felix in the side and whispered something in his ear. Felix blushed. "Fine. Two times. But that second one was for old times' sake."

Vasily blinked and decided it was better not to ask.

"Your Majesty, Your Highness," Mother said, "I plan to court Vasily. I was going to come and ask your approval today."

For all that Lilleforth wasn't Koroslova, some lessons had been so deeply ingrained they went right to the marrow of Vasily's bones, and he couldn't help the way his gut clenched in trepidation at Mother's bold declaration of his intention to court another man. He'd thought he was moving past the long-held shame about who and what he was, but his shoulders curled inward and his gaze dropped to the ground despite himself.

Mother glanced at him before reaching out and tangling his fingers in Vasily's, and it helped. Vasily took a deep breath and straightened up, giving Mother's hand a grateful squeeze.

Mother returned it.

Leopold looked between them and his face split into a grin. "Mother, have you finally found yourself a paramour?"

"Yes, sire. With your permission."

"You don't need permission. I'm quite happy for you both to court whoever you please," Leopold said. "It's none of my business."

Mother nodded. "Thank you, sire. It just seemed right to ask, what with Vasily being under me and all."

Felix let out a choked laugh.

"His *position!*" Mother said, his eyes widening. "His *position's* under me!"

Leo looked like he was trying very hard not to laugh as he said, "Give up, Mother. You're not making it any better."

"And besides, he's not under you at all," Felix said blithely.

Vasily's breath caught. Surely Felix wouldn't tell?

"I mean, seeing as he's—ow!" Felix turned and glared at Leo as he rubbed his side.

Leo glared right back before saying, "What Felix was going to say was that the royal groom is equal in authority to you. Right, Felix?"

"Of *course* that's what I was going to say! What *else* would I be going to say?" Felix rubbed at his ribcage. "I swear, it's as if you think I can't keep a—" He broke off. "Anyway, congratulations."

"Thank you, sire," Mother said, while Vasily remembered how to breathe. "How can I be of service today?"

"Oh, you know. I just like to come and visit my old stomping grounds," Felix said, wandering over to the bench where the tack was kept. He examined the coiled reins, ran a hand over the bridles where they hung on hooks with an approving hum, and picked up a riding crop, flexing it and flicking the tip softly against his palm. "There's nothing more satisfying than freshly oiled tack, is there?"

"Oh, I can think of one or two things," Leo said.

"Are you riding today, sires?" Vasily asked. "I can get the horses saddled for you in no time."

"Not today, no," Leo said. "We have other plans." The wicked smile he was giving Felix as he took the crop out of his hand reminded Vasily of a cat who intended to play with a mouse—although judging by the heated glance Felix sent back, in this case the mouse would likely enjoy it.

Leo strode through the stable door and called, "Come along, Flick."

Felix hurried after him, grinning from ear to ear.

Vasily turned to Mother. "He still has the crop. Should I go and let him know?"

"Oh, he knows, lad," Mother said, an amused expression on his face.

Vasily's brow creased in confusion. "What on earth would he need a crop for if they're not riding?"

Mother raised an eyebrow, and Vasily had a sudden recollection of something he'd seen late at night in the stables back home when he was younger. His face heated as the pieces fell into place. "*Oh*," he said. He paused, Mother watching him intently, and finally said, "Well, that explains why they're not riding today."

Mother grinned, and Vasily couldn't help but feel like he'd passed some sort of test. Turning, Mother settled his hands, warm and enticing, on Vasily's hips. "Since they're not taking the horses out today, shall we? We'll go after lunch, give them a good run." He stepped closer, his voice low in Vasily's ear. "We could go to that little grove of trees."

Vasily's pulse quickened. "The one where people go to, um, canoodle?"

"To canoodle," Mother agreed, his breath warm against the side of Vasily's throat. "Would you like that?"

"Yes," Vasily said, voice hoarse. "I'd like that very much." He tilted his head back to lean in and capture Mother's lips in a soft kiss simply because he could. Mother kissed him back, tender and all-consuming, and it was only because they heard the clatter of boots on cobbles that they parted. Mother looked like the cat who'd got the cream, and Vasily took a moment to appreciate the sight of the man in front of him who was everything he'd ever wanted, even if he hadn't known it—and who wanted him back.

It was all rather perfect.

Chapter Nine

Mother grunted as the gelding he was grooming sagged against him without warning. The horse had been taken out by one of the guards on a late patrol, and grooming him was Mother's last task for the evening. The beast either didn't know or didn't care that Mother wasn't there as a leaning post. Mother suspected the latter.

"Whoreson," he muttered under his breath, bracing himself against the weight, but there was no heat to it. He couldn't find it in himself to be annoyed, not when he was still floating from the afternoon he'd spent with Vasily.

They'd ridden out to the grove of trees and taken an hour out of their day to kiss and embrace, shedding their shirts in the weak winter sunlight and running their hands over bare skin. They'd both gotten hard and even gone as far as grinding against each other before Vasily had held up a hand for them to stop, worried that someone might ride by.

They'd lain there side by side, panting, and a blushing Vasily had laughed and suggested that they wait until their erections subsided before they rode back. Mother had laughed right alongside him. The sight of Vasily, flustered and grinning, had filled him with warmth and affection despite his blue balls.

And he *did* have blue balls—which was a first for him.

Mother had tried kissing a girl once when he was younger, but he hadn't seen what all the fuss was about and hadn't bothered pursuing her further. Nobody, man or woman, had ever tempted him like this. But Vasily? It was like he was cool, clear water on a summer's day, enticing and irresistible, and Mother couldn't get enough of him. It was utterly unexpected, which made it all the more intoxicating. Even the softest kisses had his insides melting, and he couldn't wait to have Vasily in his bed again—maybe even get his hands on his cock. Not that he'd press the issue, because though Mother might be inexperienced, Vasily was young and greener than the grass they'd rolled in that afternoon.

But it was undeniable that Vasily made him want to do things he'd never even thought of, and the insistence of his desire was thrilling in a way that took Mother's breath away. Even now, with a thousand pounds of horseflesh using him as a leaning post, Mother found his thoughts wandering to Vasily's bare torso, the scrape of his chest hair against Mother's fingertips, and the breathy little gasps he'd made when Mother had tugged at one nipple just to see what would happen.

The horse let out a snort when his hand stilled, and Mother grunted under his weight and gave him a gentle shove, causing the beast to move off him.

He continued with his grooming, his mind once again turning to Vasily and the way he made Mother's blood run hot and his cock twitch. The most surprising thing of all was that someone as handsome and charming as Vasily wanted Mother as much as Mother wanted him.

And *oh,* did he want him.

Vasily had thick, muscled thighs that sported the same fine golden hairs as his forearms, and Mother couldn't help but wonder how that hair might feel against his lips, if it would tickle if he were to kiss his way up the length of Vasily's thighs.

Want stirred in his belly, and he resolved that should the chance present itself, he'd kiss Vasily from head to toe, stopping at every interesting destination on the way.

He set aside the brush with a sigh and patted the horse's cheek. "There you go, lovely. All clean." The horse responded by nuzzling at Mother's face and hair, leaving a wet trail. Mother pushed the horse away, shuddering as warm drool dripped into the collar of his shirt. He grabbed a clean rag and wiped off the worst of it before gathering his equipment and stepping out of the stall. He walked the length of the stables, checking all was in order before bolting the doors and making his way to his cottage.

It was empty and quiet when he stepped inside, but he found he didn't mind it tonight. After all, it wasn't like he was planning to stay. He stripped out of his shirt and splashed his torso with water, running wet fingers through his hair to dislodge the stray bits of straw that inevitably ended up there. He looked at his clothing, wrinkling his nose at the state of it. Normally he wouldn't care, but tonight he took the time to retrieve clean trousers and a good shirt, tugging them on and smoothing his hands down his front to chase away the creases until he was satisfied that he looked respectable. Then, with a spring in his step despite the lateness of the day, he pulled the door open and walked down the path to Vasily's.

Tonight they'd sit together at dinner as a *courting couple*. And yes, they sat together most nights, but this felt different somehow—thus the clean shirt. Mother wondered if people would be able to tell they were together and if they'd care.

Jeremy would care, and Mother couldn't help his pleased smile at the thought of telling the young man that Vasily was no longer open to his attentions.

Only, *should* he tell him? Or should he leave that to Vasily? Vasily was from Koroslova, and old habits died hard. He'd been offended when he'd thought Mother wanted to keep their courting a secret, but maybe it was just that he wanted to be the one to decide.

What if, when it came to it, Vasily's upbringing had him afraid to step out with Mother after all?

When Mother reached Vasily's doorstep and knocked, the door flew open. "Mother!" Vasily beamed, then threw himself into Mother's arms and kissed him hard enough that it quite took his breath away. Mother kissed him right back, any doubts melting under the heat of their kiss.

When Vasily pulled back, his eyes bright and his face flushed, he looked Mother up and down. "You look very nice this evening."

It was then that Mother noticed that Vasily, too, had changed out of his stable-stained clothing and was sporting a fine linen shirt that wouldn't have looked out of place on the king himself. He found himself absurdly pleased. "I could say the same about you. That's a very fine shirt."

Vasily gave a shy smile. "Thank you. I just felt that, well, it's our first...outing, isn't it? And I wanted to look nice for you." He ran a hand through his long hair, which hung loose, falling around his shoulders in waves.

Mother smiled. "Aye, same. I've not courted before, but I'm fairly certain that you're not meant to have horse drool on your shirt."

Vasily laughed, the sound lighting Mother up inside, and they walked up to the castle hand in hand.

They fetched their meals and sat down at the long table. There must have been something in their posture or manner that showed something was different because Jeremy, who was already seated, looked between them with a furrowed brow. "What's this?"

Vasily tensed, biting his bottom lip and looking at Mother with a pensive expression. Mother debated ignoring the question and making Jeremy sweat, but then he recalled that for Vasily, who'd grown up in a kingdom where a dalliance like theirs was unthinkable, this must be nothing short of overwhelming. Mother suspected that just sitting by Mother's side, stiff and awkward but not making any move to distance himself, was taking all the courage Vasily had right now.

Mother could handle the rest.

He didn't answer Jeremy directly. Instead he leaned over, pressed a soft kiss to Vasily's temple, and said, "Eat up, love."

Vasily's cheeks reddened, and there was a moment's silence while the others at the table took in the sight of Mother wrapping one arm around Vasily's shoulders possessively before Jeremy said, "So, you're..."

"We're courting," Mother said firmly. He glared at the rest of the table with one eyebrow raised, daring anyone to say something about it.

Jeremy held his gaze for just a second before dropping his head to the table and giving a dramatic sigh. "Well, that's my chances down the drain then. Bugger."

"You had no chance to begin with, lad," Mother said, unable to hold back his smile. "Vasily has *taste*."

That startled a laugh out of Jeremy, and after that nobody mentioned it again, everyone turning back to their meals.

Mother didn't know whether the lack of reaction was because Lilleforth already had a king married to a prince, because Mother held a position of relative importance and was a favourite of the prince consort, or because his scowl really was that terrifying. He found he didn't care either, his attention on the way the tension drained from Vasily's frame as he leaned in closer, shooting Mother a grateful smile.

It led Mother to wonder what would have happened in Koroslova if Vasily had declared he was courting a man. Perhaps that was why he'd left in the first place.

Vasily smiled and laughed through dinner, his relief obvious.

He also kept his thigh pressed against Mother's under the table for the entire meal, sending Mother heated looks as a gentle tease. By the end of it, Mother could barely focus, all his awareness fixed on that long line of heat where there was nothing separating them except the fabric of their trousers.

His cock throbbed with unaccustomed hunger as he recalled the feel of Vasily's bare skin under his hands that afternoon as they'd kissed and cozied. He wondered if after dinner, Vasily would come back to his cottage so they could kiss and touch some more—perhaps do *more* than touch.

Mother had never felt this level of attraction to someone, and he was shocked by the strength of his desire. He wondered what it was that made Vasily different to every other person he'd met, before deciding it didn't matter.

Vasily *was* different.

And judging by the way Vasily had slipped one hand under the table and was running it up and down Mother's thigh while glancing at him from under his lashes with a coy smile, he was just as eager as Mother was to take things further. As soon as the last mouthful of cottage pie was gone, Mother picked up both of their plates and took them over to the washing-up buckets where one of the serving girls relieved him of them.

By the time he got back to the table, Vasily was standing, one hand extended. His cheeks were pink, but he held his hand out in a fair imitation of confidence. Mother pretended not to notice the slight tremor and took the proffered hand, giving it a reassuring squeeze. Vasily ducked in close and pressed his lips to Mother's in the briefest of kisses before pulling away again grinning.

Someone made a cooing sound—Cook, probably—but Mother pretended not to hear it, leading Vasily out of the kitchen with his head held high and ignoring the heat flooding his cheeks. This was all new, but that didn't mean he had any reason to be embarrassed by it—not when it meant he got to have someone as intriguing as Vasily in his life.

And intriguing really was the best way to describe him.

He *still* didn't know who Vasily was or how he'd come to be here. He only knew that he'd clearly come from a life of privilege and Mattias had been involved somehow. An unwelcome suspicion hit him, one so absurd that he almost dismissed it out of hand, except—

What had Felix meant about Vasily being his equal? Why were the king and his husband so eager to keep an eye on their new groom? What *did* Mattias have to do with it? He walked along, lost in thought.

"Bryn?"

The use of his name jerked him out of his thoughts, and Mother lifted his head to find that they'd somehow made it all the way back to Vasily's cottage while he'd been woolgathering.

"You haven't said a word the whole way here. Did I do something wrong?"

Vasily's brow was creased, and he pulled his hand out of Mother's grasp and fiddled with the sleeve of his shirt. "I'm sorry if I upset you. I shouldn't have kissed you in front of Cook."

"What? No. I like you kissing me. I was just lost in some foolishness."

Vasily's smile returned, although it was tinged with uncertainty. "Oh, good. Because I like kissing you too. But you look so fierce." He raised an eyebrow. "So, can I ask what had you looking like you stepped in fresh dog shit?"

The words were out of Mother's mouth before he could stop them. "You're not a spy, are you?"

Vasily's eyes went wide and his mouth dropped open in an *O* of shock, and Mother's heart sank into his boots—right until Vasily let out a startled laugh. "*Me?* A spy?" He started laughing properly then, hard enough that his body was folded in half with the force of his mirth. His arms wrapped around his middle, and in between making snorting noises, he gasped out, "That's—the most"—he paused to drag in a breath—"flattering thing I've ever heard! *Me!*" He hooted, and when he straightened up, there were tears running down his face. He wiped the back of one hand across his eyes. "I've never had anyone think I was clever enough to be a spy before. It's quite the compliment."

He was so entertained by the whole thing that Mother couldn't help but believe him. He found himself grinning. "I told you they were foolish thoughts."

Vasily had recovered from his fit of laughter somewhat, and now he draped his arms around Mother's neck and leaned in against him, still breathless as he buried his face in the crook of his neck. "A *spy*," he repeated, and Mother could hear the stifled laughter in his tone.

And fine, it *was* ridiculous. Now he thought about it, spies were meant to blend in, and right from the start Vasily had done everything *but*.

He ran a hand through his hair, feeling slightly sheepish, and tucked his fingertips under Vasily's jaw to draw his chin upward, not sure if he should apologise or join Vasily in his amusement. Vasily grinned at him. "I promise I'm not a spy. Although if I *was* a spy, that's just the sort of thing I would say, so perhaps I am."

He winked and leaned in for a kiss.

Mother slid one hand up Vasily's back and settled his palm at the nape of his neck, teasing Vasily's mouth open with the tip of his tongue and tilting his head so their mouths lined up better.

He was getting the hang of this.

Vasily seemed to think so too, letting out a soft moan and pulling away long enough to whisper, "Come inside?" before brushing his lips along Mother's throat in a series of featherlight kisses.

Mother's skin tingled with the echo of Vasily's touch and his heart thundered in his chest in a combination of nerves and excitement as he nodded wordlessly.

Vasily unlocked the door, and they stepped inside.

"Oh!"

Mother couldn't help the exclamation. He and Vasily mostly met at either his house or the stables, and the last time he'd been here the place had still looked somewhat sparse, as well as being in dire need of a clean and containing rather too much unwashed laundry. Now, though? It exuded warmth and cheer.

The coals glowed in the hearth, cutting through the chill of the evening and casting enough light to show that every last surface had been wiped clean. The place was free of clutter, the dust bunnies and cobwebs that had previously taken up residence in the corners had been evicted, and there was the hint of a soapy fragrance lingering in the air. "I see you've got the hang of housekeeping, then?"

Vasily laughed. "I spent two hours cleaning this afternoon because I planned to invite you over," he confessed. He stepped farther inside, Mother following him, and lit one of the lamps, bathing the cottage in a warm glow. He set the lamp on the small table, which held a jug of wine and two glasses. Next to it a haphazard arrangement of long-stemmed red flowers, the ones that grew in the meadow near the stables, had been shoved into a clay vase. Mother turned to Vasily, biting back a smile. "Are you trying to woo me with wine and flowers?"

He ducked his head, but not before Mother caught his shy smile. "Is it working?"

Mother plucked one of the flowers from the vase, touched by the tenderness of the gesture. "Course it is." He stepped up close to Vasily, holding it out to him. "I've never been wooed before."

Vasily took the flower, their fingers brushing softly, and gazed up at him, eyes wide. "Me either. Wooed anyone, I mean. But I like it."

He leaned in and pressed their mouths together, soft and sweet, and Mother licked into the seam of his mouth, chasing the taste of him. Heat ran through him and his heart beat faster when Vasily wrapped his arms around him and held him close. Mother wondered if it was normal to feel so *much* from a single kiss, before deciding he didn't care what normal was.

Vasily pulled back, his eyes dark, and laid the slightly crushed flower on the table. His gaze flicked between Mother and the jug and glasses. "Did you, um. Want a glass of wine?"

Mother shook his head. "I didn't come here for wine."

The tips of Vasily's ears turned dark pink, and he nodded in the direction of the bed. "When I cleaned, I put fresh linens on the bed. I don't want to presume anything, but—" Vasily swallowed hard, then stepped forward and settled his hands on Mother's hips. "Would you like to join me there, Bryn?"

Mother blinked, both surprised and charmed by Vasily's boldness, and at the mention of joining him in bed, his slow-burning arousal bloomed into something sharper, needier. He reached up and ran his fingers through Vasily's hair. It was like silk under his fingertips. He cupped Vasily's face in one palm. "I'd like that very much."

Letting out a shaky breath, Vasily leaned forward and Mother met him halfway, their mouths clashing in a desperate, messy tangle of teeth and tongues that was far better than it had any right to be. Vasily slid his hands from Mother's waist down to his arse, taking a moment to explore before cupping and squeezing the globes there, and the feel of fingertips digging into muscle had Mother moaning as tendrils of heat danced up his spine.

He slid his hands under the hem of Vasily's shirt and up his back, tracing the lines of muscle, and gods, how had he *ever* thought he wasn't interested in this? He shoved Vasily's shirt upward, a wordless request, and Vasily let go of him to peel the garment over his head and discard it on the floor. Mother took the chance to peel out of his own shirt. He drank in the sight of Vasily's broad chest and reached out and brushed a thumb over his nipple. Vasily gasped, making the same lovely little shocked sound he had last time Mother had touched him there.

Mother didn't hesitate to do it again and then, feeling bold, he leaned down and laved his tongue over the hardening nub. Vasily tasted faintly of soap and fresh sweat, and Mother wanted more. He took the nipple in his mouth and sucked.

"No!" Vasily stiffened and jerked back from Mother's touch as if he'd been struck by lightning.

Mother stilled, his heart racing. He straightened and cupped Vasily's face in one hand, searching for any sign of distress.

Vasily grinned at him. "That was—it was too good," he said, a little breathless, "and I was hoping to make it out of my trousers this time."

Oh.

Mother grinned back. "Well then, we'd best get them off," he said, and set to work making it happen. Vasily's lacings parted under his fingers, and at Vasily's nod Mother slid his trousers and smallclothes down to his knees.

Vasily stilled him with a hand to his shoulder, looking lost for a moment, before he tugged his trousers back up and sat in one of the wooden chairs. It took Mother a moment, but he soon realised Vasily had only sat down to remove his boots, and he promptly sat down to do the same.

When he lifted his head from tugging at his boot, he froze, dumbstruck, at the vision in front of him. His boot hit the floor with a thunk.

He'd seen Vasily naked once before, but now, with his cock standing hard and proud, his body gleaming in the lamplight, and dark lines of shadow dancing over his skin and highlighting the curves and planes, he was the most beautiful sight Mother had ever seen.

"Gods, lad," he said, voice hoarse with want.

Vasily, wearing a pleased smile, turned slightly to face him. He extended a hand, and Mother stood, pausing only to shed his trousers before taking it, his heart thundering and cock throbbing at the acres of gorgeous, smooth skin in front of him. He wanted to touch all of it.

Vasily led him to the bed and stood there uncertainly before whispering, "What would you like to do?"

It was an impossible question. How to choose when there was *so much* Mother wanted? But Vasily was looking at him with something like pleading in his gaze, and Mother never wanted to disappoint him. He closed his eyes, took several deep breaths, and made his choice.

He opened his eyes to find Vasily watching him. Stepping closer to the bed, Mother gave Vasily a gentle shove so that he was sitting on the side of it and dropped gracelessly to his knees in the vee of Vasily's thighs so that he was level with his cock. "Want to taste you." He sounded desperate even to his own ears.

Vasily's lips parted and his cock twitched, moisture beading at the tip. When he gave a jerky nod, Mother leaned in and gave a tentative lick up the shaft, catching the drip. It was warm and salty, the taste slightly musky. He licked his lips, considering, before deciding he liked it.

He ran his palms over the fine golden hairs and settled his hands on Vasily's thighs, noting the light tremor running through the thick muscle. He leaned in again and lapped at the rosy crown of Vasily's cock where it was peeking out, before taking the head in his mouth and sucking.

Vasily let out a groan that sounded almost like a prayer. He clutched at Mother's hair, his fingers flexing as his cock leaked steadily. Mother wrapped a hand around Vasily's shaft and started to stroke, and Vasily's moans grew louder.

Mother's own erection was straining, tight and hot and urgent, and he was desperate to get a hand on himself, but he didn't trust that he could do that and give Vasily the attention he deserved. So for now he concentrated on sucking and swallowing, easing another inch into his mouth and licking along the length as he worked out what Vasily liked.

What Vasily liked, it turned out, was everything.

He let out a series of little gasps and whines, every single one of them ratcheting Mother's own arousal higher, and it wasn't long before Vasily was rolling his hips, the cock in Mother's mouth throbbing hot and heavy against his tongue as Vasily chased his release.

When Mother used his other hand to cup Vasily's balls, Vasily's hips bucked up suddenly and the hand in Mother's hair tightened.

Something like satisfaction glowed warm in his chest, and he intensified his efforts, taking Vasily as far down as he could manage without choking.

Vasily cried out, "*Bryn!*" in warning, right before his cock thickened and pulsed, and Mother found himself swallowing hastily as his mouth was flooded with warm liquid.

It shouldn't have made his own cock throb like it did, but Mother couldn't deny that the sight of Vasily with his head thrown back, eyes closed, mouth open, and cheeks flushed with pleasure, was enough to bring him right to the edge.

"Gods," Vasily gasped out, his chest heaving, and then he was clutching at Mother's shoulders, pulling him to his feet and shoving him onto the bed. Mother landed on his back and Vasily scrambled to kneel between his legs. Before Mother had a chance to ask what he was doing, he found his cock surrounded by intoxicating wet heat, and *he* was the one letting out whimpers and groans as Vasily sucked and slurped and licked with no finesse at all.

Not that it mattered. Just the sight of Vasily, his lips stretched wide around Mother's cock, his golden locks tumbling over his shoulders, had Mother's blood thundering through his veins, his cock throbbing in time with his racing heartbeat. And when Vasily flicked his tongue over Mother's slit, wet and warm and teasing, Mother was lost in a wave of unrivalled pleasure. He arched his back as he reached his peak, his fingertips digging into the meat of Vasily's shoulders to stop himself from flying away while he shook and panted his way through his release, groaning with the intensity of it.

Vasily eased off Mother's softening cock, reaching up and splaying one hand over Mother's stomach and resting his head on his thigh, and they stayed just like that for a few minutes while they both recovered. Mother's bones had turned to water, and he didn't think he could move even if he'd wanted to—not that he did.

He did manage to reach down and run his fingers through Vasily's hair, though, and Vasily hummed with pleasure, his breath warm against the skin of Mother's thigh. Mother continued to play with the long strands of hair, running them through his fingers. A deep sense of satisfaction settled over him, and a smile crept onto his face as he wondered what Vasily would want to try next. There were so many things they hadn't done, and Mother had no doubt they'd get to all of them, but there was no rush. His smile widened.

He had a lover.

Chapter Ten

"Do you think they'll be long?" Vasily leaned over the railing and squinted to see if he could spot Leo and Felix yet. The royal couple had taken the horses out over two hours ago for a late afternoon ride. Thomas had followed at a distance, so Vasily wasn't worried for their safety, but the sun was hanging low in the sky. Soon enough the horizon would be streaked with pink as evening closed in, and he'd hoped to go for a walk with Mother along the water's edge so they could watch the sun sink into the ocean together.

Unfortunately, wanting to watch the sunset with his lover was hardly a good enough reason to abandon his post, and there was no way he was leaving the care of Blackbird and Shadow to someone else.

Still, it would have been a nice evening. He enjoyed Mother's company, and looked forward to the time they spent talking and laughing when they rode the horses or took walks together.

Mother, who was leaning next to him, nudged him with his elbow. "They won't be far off, and I'll help you get the horses bedded down." He gave Vasily a crooked smile. "We might miss the sunset, but we can still go for a pint after dinner. And afterwards, you can come over to mine."

That did sound nice. "So you're saying you're going to get me tipsy and take advantage of me?" he teased.

Mother raised an eyebrow. "If you're lucky, lad."

Vasily laughed, because the idea of Mother taking advantage of anyone was, well. Laughable. They'd only been courting for a few weeks, and the evenings they spent together didn't always end in spooning, but when they did, Vasily already knew that Mother would always, always check with Vasily when it came to trying new things in the bedroom. If anything, it was Vasily who pushed for more. But really, he reasoned, who could blame him when Mother was so very good at bedding him?

They'd ventured as far as kissing and touching, rubbing each other off, and sucking each other's cocks—Mother had turned out to be particularly talented in that regard. Sometimes, one of them would slip a finger that was slick with the special oil Mother had procured—the one that made everything ten times slipperier and a thousand times better—across the other's arsehole, simply because it felt incredible.

The noises Mother made were particularly intoxicating.

But generally, they were taking things slow. What they *had* done, though, had turned Vasily's world on its head. He was finding it increasingly difficult to think about anything except Mother's hands gripping his thighs as he sucked him down, Mother's mouth on his, and Mother's long, clever fingers wrapped around his cock.

Heat stirred low in his gut, and he let out a long sigh and forced himself to think of something else. The last thing he wanted was to try and groom a horse with a stiff cock in his trousers.

Mother rested a hand on his shoulder and nodded towards the horizon. "There you are, see? They're on the way back. We might make that walk after all."

Sure enough, three figures on horseback were trotting towards them. Vasily ducked into the stable, checked the feed troughs were full, and set out the brushes for both horses. The clatter of hooves let him know that the king and the prince consort had arrived, and he darted out, ready to take the reins.

Wearing a lazy smile, Leo slid from his mount first. Judging by his loose-limbed movements, Vasily suspected they'd stopped at the grove. His suspicions were confirmed when Felix dismounted and Vasily caught sight of fresh grass stains on the back of his shirt.

He flushed at the thought of two grown men fucking out in the open where anyone could see. It made butterflies swoop in his stomach, and he wasn't sure if it was from embarrassment or excitement.

He wondered what Thomas did with himself while Leopold and Felix frolicked, before deciding that he would never, ever ask.

He reached out for Blackbird's reins and Mother reached for Shadow, but Felix shook his head. "Why don't you take Thomas's mount, Mother? I'll help Vasily." Mother hesitated, but Felix was the prince consort after all, so Mother walked over to where Thomas had dismounted and led his horse over to the general stables.

"Are you sure, Flick?" King Leo leaned back against the railing, his arms folded over his chest. "Vasily is perfectly capable of doing his job, you know."

"I'm sure he'll be grateful for the help, and I miss grooming the horses," Felix said. "You don't have to wait."

"I'll walk you up to the castle, sire." Thomas stepped forward.

"Yes, go up to the castle, love. I'll be there soon," Felix said before turning his back on the king and leading Shadow into the stables without so much as a backward glance.

Leo blinked at being dismissed but he stood and, with a nod

at Vasily, strode up the pathway to the castle, Thomas at his back.

Vasily led Blackbird inside and into her stall and set about removing the saddle and bridle. Felix did the same for Shadow and they worked in tandem, and at first the only sounds were the drag of the brush and the soft huffs and snorts from the horses.

It was when Vasily was halfway along Blackbird's body that Felix spoke. "Have you told him?"

Vasily's head whipped up so fast that he smacked it into Blackbird's shoulder. "What?"

"Mother. Have you told him?"

Vasily's heart stuttered in his chest, and his voice shook. "I don't know what you mean, sire," he lied.

Felix gave a snort that would have rivalled one of the horses. "Please. Don't *sire* me. We both know who's the groom and who's the real prince here."

Vasily put a hand against Blackbird's side to steady himself. He knew he should tell Mother, but he'd been putting it off. Perhaps it was selfish, but he couldn't bear the thought of Mother treating him differently or perhaps not wanting anything to do with him at all. "Why?" he said in a low voice. "Why do I have to tell him?"

There was the sound of a curry comb hitting the tack table, and then Felix was right there in the stall with him, barely inches away. "Because," he said, voice equally quiet, "he deserves to know who, exactly, he's dallying with. And what's more, he deserves to know you're not staying." His gaze was hard. "Mother Jones is a decent man. He's not a plaything for a spoiled prince."

"No! It's not like that!" Vasily protested, but his heart sank —because it was *exactly* like that.

"Oh?" Felix challenged. "Decided to stay, have you?"

Vasily blinked against the wetness blurring his vision as the reality of his situation hit him full force. Because even if he *did* want to stay—and who was he fooling? Of course he did—it wasn't possible. Princes, even fourth sons, didn't slink off to neighbouring kingdoms and not return.

It just wasn't *done.*

"So what do you want me to do?" he asked, folding his arms over his chest in an attempt to hide how close he was to tears. "Give up the one good thing in my life?" His voice cracked, and he cursed the sign of weakness. His father would have been disgusted if he'd heard. He squeezed his eyes shut and ignored the single drop of moisture that trickled down his cheek.

Felix blinked, and his brow creased in concern. "Shit. Don't cry, Vasily." He placed a hand on Vasily's shoulder. "That's not what I mean. I don't want you to give him up. I just want Mother to know the truth before he falls even harder for you. At least then he'll know what he's dealing with."

Vasily froze. "Mother isn't falling for me," he whispered.

Felix let out a low chuckle. "He is, though. I've known Mother my whole life, and I've never known him to have a romantic entanglement. With you, though? He gazes after you like a lovesick calf. He holds your hand. He glares at anyone who looks at you sideways. He definitely has strong feelings for you."

His chest tightened, and he didn't know whether to laugh or cry. Hearing that Mother was falling for him was all well and good, but it didn't change the fact that Vasily was a prince—and that he couldn't stay. It was an impossible situation, and it was only made worse by the fact that if he was honest, Vasily was falling just as hard. He sniffled and leaned against Blackbird, hiding his face as he whispered into her coat. "He's not the only one."

Felix rested a hand on his shoulder. "So? That's a good thing, Vasily. You should tell him that you care."

Sighing, Vasily lifted his head, scrubbing the heel of his hand over his eyes. "What good would that do?"

Felix rolled his eyes. "Well, for a start, it would make him happy. And if anyone deserves to be happy, it's Mother. So you could, I don't know. Start with the fact you're besotted with him, and once he's over that, sort of...casually mention that you're royalty? And then, once he stops calling you sire and hyperventilating, you can both figure out how you're going to stay together."

Vasily snorted. "Yes, because obviously that's going to happen."

"Why can't it?" Felix asked, the corners of his mouth quirking up.

"Because it *can't*," Vasily mumbled, staring at the floor.

Felix lifted his chin with one long finger. "Look me in the eye and tell me that a prince can't fall in love with a groom and live happily ever after. I *dare* you."

Vasily blinked as a flicker of hope ignited in his chest, but he shoved it down, twisting his head away from Felix's touch. "That's *you*. That's Lilleforth. It's different for me."

Is it, though?

Vasily tried and failed to ignore the voice in his head. He couldn't help but ask, "If I did want to stay, how would that even work? I can't exactly disappear from Koroslova. People would notice."

Felix ran one hand through his hair and rested the other on Blackbird's nose, petting her absently. "I don't have an answer for you. But Mother should know who you are, at the very least. And then maybe the pair of you can figure something out. They do say two heads are better than one."

Vasily let out a gusty sigh, knowing Felix was right. "I'm going to tell him," he said. "It's just...finding the right time."

Felix nodded. "I understand, trust me. But don't leave it too long. Mother's a tender soul under all that bluster, and he has no tolerance for deception."

Blackbird chose that moment to turn her head and nuzzle the side of Vasily's face, and Felix laughed at his outraged squawk. Then, while Vasily was wiping his face, he moved back into Shadow's stall, and before long Vasily heard the sound of long, smooth brush strokes as Felix finished grooming his horse. He picked up his equipment and did the same, his hands moving automatically over Blackbird's coat as he turned over what Felix had said.

He *did* need to tell Mother who he was—that was indisputable. But he had months and months before he even had to think about leaving, so it wasn't like he had to break it to him right this minute.

He finished up with Blackbird and stepped out of the stall just as Mother rapped on the wooden doorframe. "All done?" he asked, stepping inside.

"All done," Vasily said, unable to hold back his smile.

Mother stepped closer and wrapped his arms around him. "We can still take that walk and watch the sunset if you'd like." He pressed a soft kiss to Vasily's temple.

"You know, *my* husband's never taken me for a walk at sunset," Felix said, strolling out of Shadow's stall. "He's obviously not a born romantic like you, Mother."

Mother jerked back, but Vasily got the feeling it was more in surprise at Felix's appearance than anything, and he was quick to slip his palm into Vasily's. "Begging your pardon, sire, but I disagree," Mother said. "His Majesty changed the laws of an entire kingdom to marry you. I think he must be at least a *little* bit romantic."

Felix sighed. "I suppose. And I've *told* you, stop calling me sire."

"Shan't, sire. You're prince consort now. It's only proper to use your title."

Vasily's stomach gave an odd little flip-flop. *This* was why he didn't want to reveal his identity yet. Was it so wrong to want to enjoy being just Vasily for a little while longer, instead of being feted as a prince?

Felix tilted his head. "So, as the prince consort, you'll respect my authority and title—*except* when I ask you to use my name and not my title? That makes no sense."

"Not much about royal protocol does...*sire*," Mother said with a shrug.

Felix laughed, and Vasily got the sense that they'd had this conversation many times before.

"Enjoy your walk," Felix said, and then he was gone, striding the path up to the castle, the grass stains on his back a stark contrast to the crisp white linen of his shirt.

As they watched him go, Vasily said, "He has a point, though. Why call him sire when he's asked you not to? Surely his wishes override protocol?"

Mother grinned and bumped his shoulder against Vasily's. "It does Flick good not to get his own way all the time, lad. Otherwise he'd end up with his head fair up his arse, and he'd be insufferable."

That startled a laugh out of Vasily, and he hoped it meant that perhaps Mother wouldn't be *too* upset at finding out that Vasily was a prince after all.

But that didn't mean he was ready to tell him.

~

They made it down to the ocean just before the sun dipped below the horizon, and sat together on the low stone harbour wall near where the fishing boats were moored. They watched as the sky turned a glorious array of colours before the darkness swallowed them up and night fell. Mother had one arm wrapped firmly around Vasily's waist, holding him steady, and the heat and weight of his arm was a welcome comfort. Vasily had mostly recovered from the shocking—to him, at least—revelation that he didn't want to leave and that he might feel more for Mother than he'd previously thought. Having his lover hold him like he was something precious was helping to chase away the last traces of his unease.

Besides, he was a fan of cuddling generally where Mother was concerned.

"Still want that pint?" Mother murmured. "Or shall we head back?" He leaned in and nuzzled at Vasily's ear, his breath a warm contrast to the crisp night air, and it was far nicer than when Blackbird had done it earlier. Mother had discovered early on that Vasily had a sensitive spot at the side of his throat, and when he grazed his lips against the skin just like he was doing now, it generally meant he had one thing on his mind.

Vasily shivered with anticipation. "Home, please?"

Mother clambered to his feet and then held out a hand, keeping Vasily steady as he stood. "Careful of that edge, lad," he said in warning, just like he always did. Vasily took two steps away, just like he always did. Mother's concern about his safety around water was both understandable and touching, and Vasily never mocked him for it.

As they walked back, he noticed that most of the stalls and shopfronts were decorated with long strips of brightly coloured cloth hanging across the front, and it looked like the cobbles had been swept clean. "What's the bunting for?" he asked Mother, nodding at the haphazard flags.

"Blessing of the Fleet tomorrow, lad," Mother said. "Happens every year on the first day of spring. The king rides down, and the bishop comes and prays for good catches and safe passage. It's a good day for the stallholders."

Vasily nodded—he'd known they were saddling the royal mounts for tomorrow. This must be why.

As they walked back through the cobbled streets hand in hand, Vasily wondered how many more times they'd get to do this once he told Mother the truth. Maybe it wouldn't make a difference, or maybe Mother would reject him as a liar and a fraud—or worse, call him sire and refuse to look him in the eye, let alone touch him.

Vasily desperately hoped for the former, but he wasn't foolish enough to count on it. And before he was willing to risk losing Mother, there were things he wanted to try—*one* thing, specifically. Then, if it all went awry, at least he wouldn't be left wondering what he was missing.

His stomach swooped and swirled at the very idea of asking, torn between worry that Mother would say no, or worse, that he'd say yes and then it wouldn't turn out to be what Vasily wanted after all. But he pushed those fears aside and steeled his resolve.

They approached the row of cottages and stopped in front of Vasily's front door. Normally there was a moment of to and fro while they decided who was staying with who, but not tonight. Not with what Vasily had in mind. He cleared his throat. "Will you come in?"

Something in his tone must have alerted Mother that this was different to his usual invitation. He raised an eyebrow, and Vasily felt the weight of his stare. "Did you have something in mind, Vas?" Mother's gaze was dark with want, and he wondered if Mother was thinking the same thing he was.

He hoped so.

At a loss for words, he pulled Mother in for a kiss. The familiarity of it, the way Mother's hands roamed over Vasily's back and sides, his touch both tender and desperate, ignited a fire in his belly even as his heart thundered in his chest. He broke the kiss.

"I want..." He faltered.

Mother dropped his hands to his sides before pressing their foreheads together, and his voice was gravel rough when he said, "Anything, Vas."

And with those two words, Vasily knew that he *could* ask for anything and Mother would do his utmost to give it to him. He trusted Mother, and he *wanted* this.

Still, his voice shook the tiniest bit when he clasped Mother's hands in his, looked him in the eye, and asked.

"Make love to me, Bryn?"

Chapter Eleven

"*Make love to me, Bryn?*"

Even though Mother had suspected what Vasily wanted to ask, the words still echoed around his skull, ringing loudly in his ears as he struggled to comprehend them.

Vasily's eyes were wide and the moonlight showed a flush on his cheeks, one that Mother happened to know spread all the way down his chest when he was aroused. The taste of him still lingered on Mother's tongue, and his hands were cool where his grip had tightened on Mother's fingers.

It was obvious that Vasily was as nervous as a mouse in a barn full of cats, but he'd asked anyway, and the very idea that he was willing to take that step with Mother was overwhelming.

He couldn't imagine refusing, not when he wanted the same thing.

Mother wrapped his arms around Vasily's back and pulled him close, nuzzling at that spot under his ear that made him squirm in the best of ways before leaving a trail of kisses down the side of his throat. "Gods, yes." Mother breathed the words against his skin, and Vasily relaxed in his arms.

Lifting his head, Mother pressed their mouths together. Vasily kissed him back with an urgency that hadn't been there before, his tongue sliding along the seam of his mouth. Mother opened for him, letting their tongues dance and tease and twist together. His arousal grew as he pictured them tangled in the bedsheets together, skin pressed against naked skin, oil-slicked fingers teasing at his arse—

Wait.

He pulled back, his breathing shallow, and tried to gather himself. A shiver ran through him.

"Bryn?" Vasily peered at him in the dim light, a crease appearing between his brows.

"It's bloody cold," Mother said to cover his confusion. "We should get inside before our bollocks freeze off."

Vasily grinned at that. "Good idea. Frozen bollocks could play havoc with our plans." He unlocked the door and stepped inside, shedding his coat and moving over to the fireplace to stoke the flames to life, oblivious to the fact that Mother was having a major personal revelation.

Mother followed him inside, stripping out of his own coat and dropping it on top of Vasily's on the kitchen chair as his mind whirled. He'd never really thought about being fucked—hadn't thought much about sex at all before Vasily.

But once again, it seemed the usual rules didn't apply where Vasily was concerned, because now he'd *started* thinking about it, he couldn't stop. The idea of Vasily on top of him, pressing him into the mattress and fucking him deep, had him hardening in his trousers. But he knew that wasn't what Vasily had meant when he'd invited him inside. How to suggest it without it sounding like a rejection of what Vasily was offering?

"Bryn?" Vasily said softly, trailing a fingertip down Mother's cheek to get his attention. "Is this all right?"

Mother blinked and forced a smile. "Aye. But a man's allowed to be nervous."

Vasily bit his bottom lip, betraying his own nerves. "Me too. I mean, I have no idea if I'll even *like* a cock in my arse."

Well, if that wasn't an opening, Mother didn't know what was. He took a deep breath, and before he lost his nerve, said, "But I might."

Vasily tilted his head. "Might what?"

Mother could feel his cheeks heating, but he held Vasily's gaze. Tell the truth and shame the devil, wasn't that what they said? "Like it. A cock. *Your* cock. In me."

Vasily's eyes widened. "Really? You'd let me..."

He gave a terse nod. "If you wanted," he added, only too aware that it might not be something Vasily was interested in.

"That would be—" Vasily broke off, apparently lost for words, but his face split into a delighted grin that showed just how much he liked the idea, and the tightness in Mother's chest eased.

"We can figure it out as we go, like always." He reached out and gripped Vasily by the hips, drawing him close so that Vasily's hardness was pressed against his own, and whispered, "I like the sound of both, if I'm honest."

Vasily let out a soft whimper that went straight to Mother's cock before reaching up to thread his fingers through Mother's hair and hold him in place as he kissed him, hot and hungry.

Mother tugged Vasily's shirt out from his trousers and slid his palms up over his ribs and down his spine. Vasily mirrored the action, but he didn't stop at the dip of Mother's spine, sneaking a hand into the waistband of Mother's trousers and cupping his arse, making heat pool low in his belly.

A moan escaped him, and Vasily's mouth curved up into a smile against his. He pulled back, face flushed and eyes bright, and started steering them haphazardly across the room towards the bed, his steps unsteady. They might have made faster progress if Vasily hadn't kept stopping to press hot, open-mouthed kisses down the length of Mother's throat, but Mother wasn't going to stop him, not when every kiss had his heart racing and his cock filling.

The back of Mother's knees hit the mattress and he let himself fall backward. Vasily landed on top of him, balancing on his elbows, and leaned in for a proper kiss.

He was all hard muscle and heat, and the weight of him felt so very right that it would have been easy to get swept away in the touch and the taste and the heat of him. Before that happened, though, Mother shoved at Vasily's chest and gasped out, "Wait."

Vasily tensed. "Do you want to stop?" His disappointment was palpable.

"*Stop*?" Mother propped himself up on his elbows, giving a breathless laugh. "Gods, no. I just need to get my boots off, and *you* need to lock the door. I don't plan on us being disturbed."

"Oh!" Vasily brightened, and his enthusiasm was endearing enough that the last of Mother's nervousness melted in the face of it.

Vasily hurried to lock the door, and they both undressed hastily. Mother pulled his shirt over his head, and when he emerged from the temporary darkness, it was to find a naked Vasily. Biting his lip, Vasily ran his hands down his chest and across his stomach before wrapping a hand around his cock and stroking himself in an obvious display.

He was glorious.

"Gods but you're pretty," Mother growled out, wondering if the sight of Vasily naked would ever fail to thrill him. Probably not. He looked him up and down, taking in the flex of his muscles, the curve of his belly, and the proud jut of his cock. The head peeked out of his fist, shiny with precum, and Mother licked his lips.

It was ridiculous, but he had a sudden urge to put on a show of his own. What did it matter that he wasn't as young as he once had been? Vasily obviously found him attractive, if his raging erection was anything to go by. Mother slid onto the bed and settled himself against the headboard, his legs splayed wide, his knees bent, and his heels pressing into the mattress. After licking his palm, he took hold of his cock and dragged his hand up the length, letting out a low groan.

Vasily's mouth dropped open, and satisfaction ran through Mother. "Oh fuck, Bryn," Vasily said breathlessly, crawling up the bed and batting Mother's hand away. He replaced it with his own, the heat of his palm setting Mother's nerves alight, his strokes firm and sure.

"Hnngh," Mother gritted out, bucking his hips up into the touch. Vasily grinned as he lowered his head and licked a stripe up Mother's length before taking both his hand and mouth away.

Mother whimpered as he fucked up into thin air, and Vasily's smile, which was laced with pure mischief, widened. "Gods, I love the sounds you make when you're desperate." He locked one hand in place on Mother's hip so he couldn't move, and flicked his tongue across the head of his cock in a series of kitten licks.

Mother thought he might lose his mind.

"Don't tease," he rasped out. "Please."

"I won't," Vasily said, his warm breath ghosting over Mother's damp cockhead and making a liar out of him before he mercifully pulled back and sat up. He ran a hand through his long hair and swallowed. "Shall I get the oil?"

Mother nodded before rolling onto his stomach and pulling his knees up under himself to make things easier. He might not have done this before, but he'd heard enough talk to know the mechanics of it all.

Vasily drew in a sharp breath, loud in the silence, and then there was a muttered, "Fuck, fuck, *fuck,*" as oil—too *much* oil—ran down the crack of Mother's arse, dripping over his balls and onto the sheets. He turned his head to find Vasily grinning sheepishly, his cheeks aflame as he held up the near-empty flask. "Lost my grip."

Mother couldn't hold back a grin of his own. "Well, you're a decent size. We'll probably need it all." He settled on his elbows again, his head hanging down.

Vasily traced a slick finger around Mother's hole, spreading the oil and teasing the nerve endings there. When he did it again, pressing in slightly this time, Mother couldn't hold back the broken moan that escaped him as his body lit up, pleasure racing through him.

If the touch of a finger had him falling apart, how was he ever supposed to last long enough for Vasily to fuck him?

Vasily gripped one hip and slid his fingers down the crack of Mother's arse and back up again, slowly and carefully, increasing the pressure with every pass until finally, one fingertip eased inside and all the breath left Mother's lungs.

He tensed and Vasily stilled as he adjusted.

"Is this all right?" Vasily whispered, his voice strained.

Mother gave a sharp nod and Vasily resumed moving, settling into a steady rhythm that soon had Mother rocking back into the touch, greedy for more.

It was better than anything he'd imagined.

As if reading his mind, Vasily said, "Another one?"

"Please," Mother gasped.

He wasn't prepared for the stretch and sting of two fingers and he had to take a few deep breaths, but then the momentary pain faded and turned into something else, a pleasant fullness that made heat pool in his gut and his cock throb.

There was a gentle tug at his rim every time Vasily withdrew his fingers only to plunge them in again, and it sent shivers running down Mother's spine. He couldn't help the breathy moans that escaped him as new sensations washed over him, building in intensity with every twist of Vasily's clever fingers—strange, yes, but oh, so *good*.

He ached with need as he imagined how much better Vasily's thick length would feel sliding inside of him, and he didn't want to wait any longer. "I need you in me," he blurted out before he could talk himself out of it.

Vasily paused, breathing heavily. "Bryn—"

"Please, please," Mother chanted, unable to think, barely able to speak, all his focus on the foreign ache in his arse that just made him want more.

The fingers disappeared, leaving him far too empty, but it was only for a moment. Then Vasily was slotting himself in the space behind him, draping himself over Mother's spine and pressing a kiss to the nape of his neck. "Are you sure?"

Mother spread his knees wider in response, slipping a hand underneath himself and stroking his cock as he took several deep breaths, caught between nervousness and need.

Vasily kissed his way across his shoulders before kneeling up behind him and settling the head of his cock against Mother's loosened hole. He laid one hand on the small of Mother's back and pressed forward. There was a moment where Mother thought it wasn't going to work, that they'd done this all wrong, but then Vasily *pushed* and Mother breathed out at the right time, and there was nothing but the overwhelming stretch of Vasily's cock sliding smoothly into his arse.

The initial ache was intense but Mother panted through it with fast, shallow breaths as he closed his eyes, adjusting to the feel of his body being invaded.

Not invaded, he corrected himself. *Not when you invited it.*

"Oh gods," Vasily said, his voice catching—and then he started to thrust.

The push-pull of hard, slippery flesh felt better than it had any right to, and Mother stroked himself faster, arching his back. The movement changed the angle of Vasily's cock, and he brushed over something inside Mother. The resulting flash of heat and pleasure shocked him with its intensity, making him throw back his head and let out a shout.

Vasily made a soft noise of surprise, and then his hands tightened on Mother's hips and he thrust forward again, rubbing over the same spot.

Balls tight and cock aching, Mother tensed as his release loomed like a storm cloud, dark and heavy. His arse clenched around Vasily's cock and Vasily gasped, "*Oh!*" before letting out a low grunt, slamming his hips forward, and collapsing against Mother's back, panting.

The heat of his breath against Mother's skin along with his cock brushing against that magic spot inside was enough to tip Mother over the edge, his hips stuttering as he fucked into his fist, fast and desperate, and spilled all over the bedding.

Mother shuddered and shook through his release, which seemed to last forever. When even his own touch was too much to bear, he pulled his hand away, collapsing against the mattress in a boneless heap as Vasily followed him.

Mother had always thought there was nothing better than being on horseback, that it felt as close to flying as a man could get. How wrong he'd been.

This. This was flying.

He lay there, blanketed by the heat and weight of Vasily's body against his, and drifted.

It could have been minutes or hours, Mother wasn't sure. Eventually, though, Vasily eased out of him and pressed a kiss to the shell of his ear, the simple gesture of affection making him shiver. Mother gradually became aware of the ache in his arse and the odd, empty feeling where Vasily's cock had been lodged.

He squirmed under his Vasily-shaped blanket, and Vasily hummed and kissed the nape of his neck before rolling to one side and resting a hand on Mother's back.

Mother turned to look at him and found Vasily wearing a dazed expression. Well-fucked was the word that sprang to mind, and Mother had no doubt that he looked just as wonderfully overwhelmed. Vasily blinked at him and tensed slightly, his brow creasing with an unspoken question.

Reaching out, Mother clumsily brushed Vasily's blond locks away from his face. "We'll be doing that again."

Vasily bit his lip, and Mother wanted to reach out and tug it from between his teeth. "So it was…"

"Perfect," Mother said firmly. "It was perfect, Vas."

Vasily smiled widely, his relief obvious. "So you'd really do it again?"

Mother grinned back. "Not for a bit. My arse aches something fierce, and if I have to ride in the morning, I'll feel it, but in a day or two? Abso-bloody-lutely."

Letting out a contented sigh, Vasily said, "Oh good. I was worried because I barely lasted at all."

Mother snorted. "That makes two of us."

He rolled to face Vasily and wrinkled his nose in distaste when the change in position had his arse leaking. "Gods, that'll take some getting used to." He levered himself into a sitting position.

Vasily stared at him, uncomprehending, before realisation dawned. He scrambled out of bed and over to the washbasin, coming back with a damp cloth. "Lie down," he ordered. "Let me clean you up."

Mother didn't argue. Lying down again honestly sounded wonderful, his limbs still heavy from his orgasm. He yelped a moment later when the cold cloth touched his skin. Vasily was infinitely gentle when he wiped him down, though, cleaning away the mess of oil and seed, and the coolness of the cloth against his hole was a welcome relief that had him sighing into the pillow.

Once he'd cleaned him up, Vasily pressed a series of kisses up the length of his spine, and Mother melted into the mattress. Vasily stretched out alongside him, pulled the quilt up over them, and wrapped himself around Mother's back with a happy sigh. "You're staying, right?" he asked quietly, his hold tightening like he thought Mother might try and escape.

Mother nestled back into his arms. "Nowhere I'd rather be, lad."

Vasily might have mumbled a reply, but Mother didn't hear it, already drifting into a dreamless slumber.

Chapter Twelve

Vasily tried and failed to hide his grin at the hitch in Mother's step as he walked across the stable yard.

Mother arched a brow as he leaned over the wooden railing, propping one leg on the lower bar. "Something funny, lad?"

"Nothing at all," Vasily lied, smirking.

Mother grinned back. "It's fine, lad. Laugh away." His smile faded and a look of naked affection replaced it. "Last night was worth the ache. It was something special."

He wasn't sure how to respond to that. Did he say, "You're welcome"? Ask for pointers for next time? Offer to return the favour?

Last night *had* been special. He'd spilt the oil and it had been over far too fast, but for all that, he wouldn't change any of it. Nothing had ever felt as good as the clench of Mother's arse around his cock. Combined with the noises Mother had made, Vasily didn't think he could be blamed for his lack of stamina—not when Mother had fallen apart so beautifully.

It had been nothing short of magical.

"Vas?"

Mother's smile had faded, and Vasily realised he'd been silent for far too long. "I was just thinking of how beautiful you looked when you came," he said.

The tips of Mother's ears turned pink. He flapped his hand in a dismissive gesture and huffed out, "Flatterer," but his smile was back in full force.

Vasily stepped closer, leaning over the railing and pressing a kiss to Mother's cheek. "I mean it. You're gorgeous."

There was the sound of a throat clearing, and Vasily spun on his heel to find Janus Hobson, the captain of the guard, observing them. "What is it about the stables that always has people kissing?" he asked, his mouth curving up.

"Perhaps we just like horsing around," Mother replied without missing a beat.

Janus laughed. "Well, when you're done horsing around, I came to remind you that Flick and Leo's horses need to be ready just before noon, and Davin's too. They're heading into the city for the Blessing of the Fleet, so I'll need six horses for the guards as well."

"Any six?" Mother asked, all business.

"Thomas and I will take the usual, but otherwise any of them are fine. It's all pomp and ceremony anyway. I really don't think they're under much threat from a game of Catch the Herring."

Vasily thought of the fluttering strips of bunting he'd noticed adorning the shopfronts last night as they'd walked through town. He hadn't realised it was quite such an occasion. "Is it a big event?" he asked.

"We're a port city. It's practically a holiday," Mother said. "Why do you think I've let the stable boys bunk off today?"

Vasily looked around. Well, that explained the empty stables.

"There are players and jesters and all sorts," Mother continued. "The king rides at the head of the procession, followed by members of court, and then the bishop. Once the bishop has blessed the fleet, the fishermen all receive a gold coin from the royal purse for luck, and then it's mostly eating and drinking for the day. There's even a fair with games. It's meant to be for the youngsters, but plenty of adults enjoy it as well."

"Felix is bellyaching already because he won't be able to go and try his hand at the ring toss on account of being a prince now," Janus said with a grin. "I told him not to expect any sympathy from his mother and me. That's what he gets for marrying royalty."

"Aye, it would take a lot to get me involved with that sort of dog and pony show," Mother said with a shake of his head.

Vasily remained silent and did his best to ignore the lead ball that had lodged in the pit of his stomach. Mother was only saying that because he didn't know, he reminded himself. When it came down to it, perhaps he'd decide Vasily was worth it.

He could only hope.

"Is the crown prince excited?" he asked in an attempt to change the subject.

"Davin? He can't wait. He was up at dawn, and he's spent the morning preening in the mirror, making sure he's every inch the handsome prince." Janus chuckled.

"Like father, like son?" Mother said with a wry smile.

"Peas in a pod," Janus agreed. "But I will say he's very diligent in his duties. If you ask me, I credit that to his time in the stables learning to do a day's work."

Mother chuffed out a laugh. "He was slow to start, but he turned out to be a decent lad in the end."

"Most princes are, underneath the formality and bollocks," Janus said, looking directly at Vasily.

A sharp gasp escaped him against his will. Of *course* the captain of the guard knew who he was. But Janus wouldn't tell, would he?

He sent a silent, wide-eyed plea and received an almost imperceptible nod in return, which he took to mean his secret was safe. He drew in a shaky breath that had Mother turning to him, brow creased.

"Are you all right, Vasily?"

"Fine," he lied and pasted on a smile. "Are we going to the Blessing?"

Mother gave him a shy smile. "If you'd like. I thought we could make an afternoon of it."

"Yes, please." Vasily brushed a stray bit of hay off Mother's sleeve, just as an excuse to touch him.

Janus ran a hand down the back of his neck. "I'd better get back. I still have to choose who today's guard of honour will be. Apparently, there are quite a few clamouring for the chance."

"You should pick Jeremy," Vasily said. He still felt bad about abandoning the young man for Mother, even though that hadn't been his original intention.

Janus smiled. "Maybe I will. He's a handsome lad. He'd certainly look fine in his dress livery."

"He would," Vasily agreed.

Mother's mouth tightened, and he muttered something under his breath that sounded a lot like *"Pudding-headed pretty boy."*

He probably shouldn't have been as pleased as he was at Mother's jealousy, but Vasily still had to bite back a grin as he rubbed a hand over Mother's shoulder. "He's not nearly as handsome as you, mind."

He was rewarded with a reluctant smile and a flush of colour to Mother's cheeks.

Janus cleared his throat. "I'll be back later. I have to go and get into my own dress uniform." He wrinkled his nose and sighed. "All those damn buttons."

Vasily thought about his own dress robes with their rows of tiny fastenings and wondered, when the time came, if he'd be able to get used to wearing them again. He pushed the thought away.

When Janus had left, Vasily and Mother worked side by side to make sure the horses were groomed and fed and the stables clean. It took most of the morning, and the process was definitely slowed down by Vasily's propensity to stop and steal kisses. Then again, Mother didn't object.

When it came time to prepare the horses for the parade, Mother selected the six mounts with the most placid temperaments. "There'll be crowds and noise and all sorts," he said. "We want horses that won't get skittish."

Vasily nodded, familiar with the hoopla that accompanied such an event—although in his case, his experience was limited to being the one on horseback.

They prepared the horses, making sure their saddles gleamed and their tack was spotless. Once they were ready, Mother led the mounts out into the courtyard, and while they waited for them to be collected, he tended to the manes on the royal horses.

Vasily watched, fascinated, as Mother made soothing noises while his big, clever hands twisted the hair into smooth, even braids. He'd never suspected Mother possessed such a skill, and he was torn between admiration and envy.

"I wish my hair looked like that," he said wistfully. He hadn't even managed a ponytail this morning, choosing an extra ten minutes wrapped around a sleeping Mother over personal grooming, and his hair hung loose and messy.

Mother stepped closer, wiping his palms on his shirt. "We have time. I could do it?" He looked almost hopeful.

Warmth settled in Vasily's chest as he imagined Mother tending to him in that way. "I'd like that."

Mother dragged a low wooden stool into a corner of the courtyard, and Vasily sat down. Standing behind him, Mother ran his fingers through Vasily's hair, massaging his scalp. Vasily couldn't hold back a moan.

Mother chuckled. "I'll remember to do that again later." His hands stilled. "I don't have a brush, so it won't be perfect."

"I don't care," Vasily said. "Anything's an improvement on this." He ran a hand through the mess.

"I don't know," Mother said, voice low as his hands worked. "I like it like this. It looks like you've just had a tumble in the sheets with some lucky soul."

Vasily's face heated. "I think I was the lucky one."

Mother hummed, tilting Vasily's head this way and that. He sat loose and relaxed with his eyes closed as Mother tugged gently on the strands of his hair and arranged them to his satisfaction. It seemed barely any time had passed before his hands disappeared and Mother declared, "Done."

Vasily opened his eyes to find Mother standing in front of him holding a hand mirror. "Where did that come from?"

"Davin," Mother said. "Kept it stashed in the tack room in case he needed to make himself pretty for one of his lasses." He extended the mirror. "You look like you'd fit in up at the castle, even if I say so myself. What do you think?"

Vasily took the glass, looked at himself, and swallowed.

Mother was right. Despite the lack of a brush, he'd done an excellent job of taming the waves in Vasily's hair, pulling them back to create a long, smooth braid and tying it with a leather strip, and the image he saw in the mirror wasn't Vasily the groom. It was Vasily Petrov, Prince of Koroslova, fifth in line for the throne.

He'd forgotten he could look like that—was *meant* to look like that.

He found himself straightening his spine and tensing, the years of *shoulders back, chin out, no slouching* that had been drummed into him as instinctive as ever.

Some of his disquiet must have shown because Mother crouched in front of him, brow creased. He winced as he did so, and the reminder of last night loosened something in Vasily's chest. Here, at least, he could still be himself. Here, he was just

Vasily the groom, who was lucky enough to have a handsome older lover.

Mother tilted his head, considering, before he reached out a hand and smoothed it over Vasily's hair. Then he tugged at the tie and pulled it off, running his fingers through the braid and freeing the strands of hair until they once again fell in loose waves around Vasily's shoulders.

Vasily felt the tension leave him along with the tightness of the braid. "Better," Mother said quietly. "I prefer you undone."

His gaze was so open, so affectionate, that Vasily couldn't help himself. He surged forward, pulling Mother in for a savage, heated kiss. It was uncoordinated at first, but then Mother wrapped one broad palm around the nape of Vasily's neck, angling his head and making the kiss more, better.

He wasn't sure when, exactly, Mother pulled him to his feet, but he went willingly, sliding his hands over Mother's shoulders, the flex of muscle under his fingertips sending a thrill through him. Mother walked him backward until he was pressed against the stable door, and the kisses turned syrupy-slow and lazy as Vasily closed his eyes and let himself enjoy the rasp of stubble. He inhaled Mother's scent, an intoxicating mixture of hay and fresh sweat that made Vasily want nothing more than to get him naked and kiss every inch of that lean, muscled frame.

He was just contemplating slipping a hand inside Mother's trousers and seeing what sort of noises he could pull from him when they were disturbed by the steady rhythm of boots marching on the cobblestones.

The guards were here.

Mother straightened and stepped away—but not before pressing one last kiss to Vasily's cheek and tucking a lock of hair behind his ear, the casual affection in the gesture somehow making it more intimate than anything they'd done the night before.

"Horses ready, Vasily?" King Leopold asked cheerfully as he

walked into the yard flanked by Felix, Davin, and the guards, resplendent in their dress uniforms. "Of course, sire," Vasily said, hastening to untie Blackbird from the hitching rail and leading her over to the king. Mother did the same with Shadow.

The king and prince consort were wearing royal blue surcoats with gold embroidery along the cuffs and collar, crisp linen shirts, and fitted black trousers. Matching gold coronets and fur-trimmed capes topped off the ensemble.

Felix reached up and fidgeted with his coronet and Leo sighed, reaching out and pulling his hand away. "Leave it, sweetheart."

The prince rolled his eyes. "I think I preferred being a groom," he grumbled.

"Apologies, sire, that job's been filled. You'll have to stay married to His Majesty," Mother said, and Vasily bit back a smile.

"Are we going?" Davin interrupted. He looked every inch the crown prince in his own outfit of surcoat, cape, and coronet. His face was wreathed in smiles, and his youthful excitement was obvious. Without waiting for an answer, he untied his mount and hoisted himself into the saddle.

"We really should get moving," Leo agreed, mirroring Davin's actions. Side by side, father and son were remarkably alike.

There was a flurry of activity as everyone mounted and got the horses into formation before walking out of the stable yard. It was, Vasily knew from his own experiences, a pale imitation of the procession that would make its way into the city once all the other participants had assembled at the castle gates.

The last horse turned the corner of the path, hooves echoing on stone, and then it was just the two of them. Mother looked at him with a satisfied smile. "That's us done for the day, at least until the horses are back tonight." He stepped closer, one hand settling on the curve of Vasily's lower back. "Shall we walk down to the harbour?"

Vasily *did* want to go to the Blessing, but right now he could think of other things they could be doing. "We could," he said, pressing his mouth to Mother's ear. "But I was thinking. It's not often we get an hour to ourselves during the day. We could make the most of it." He leaned in, licking a long, delicate stripe along the jut of Mother's collarbones.

Mother's hand flexed against the fabric of his shirt, and his voice was hoarse when he said, "That. Let's do that."

∼

They made it in time for the Blessing—just. It turned out that the amount of time it took for a royal procession to assemble and walk sedately down to the harbour while stopping to wave at the crowds was *exactly* the amount of time it took to suck someone off, have him return the favour, catch one's breath, and then both hurry, laughing, down to the waterfront.

Vasily was breathless when they arrived, and he let Mother lead him through the crowds, ducking and weaving around people expertly until he found them a good spot to watch from, biding Vasily to wait there. He stared around wide-eyed. It was a very different experience, being one of the people who were jostling for a glimpse of the king and not the one on horseback waving and nodding.

Both sides of the street were filled with people all waiting to see the royal couple, their bodies packed close. Some of them refused to budge an inch and others milled about, waving to friends before wandering off to join them. Children ran back and forth laughing while their parents watched on, and a small boy barrelled into Vasily's kneecaps, landing on his backside with a plop. He stared up before scrambling to his feet and scampering away.

It was noisy and packed, chaotic and overwhelming, and Vasily loved it.

There were street vendors selling an array of foods that ranged from candies and dried fish to unidentified meat on sticks, pastries, and hot balls of dough dusted with sugar. Vasily's mouth watered at the smells and sounds of cooking, and he recalled that they'd skipped lunch in favour of more interesting activities. Just then Mother appeared beside him holding out a twist of paper that smelled heavenly. He opened it to find the sugared dough balls.

"Thought maybe you'd worked up an appetite," Mother said with a grin.

Vasily moaned when he took a bite, his mouth filling with a heady combination of crispy warmth and sweetness. He shoved the rest of the treat into his mouth, ignoring the fact it was far too hot and chewing rapidly as he chased more of the taste. "Gods, that's good. Thank you."

"My pleasure, lad." The way Mother's smile lit up his face made Vasily want to kiss him despite being in a public place. After glancing around, his heart pounding, he stood on his tiptoes and pressed a chaste kiss to Mother's lips.

The part of him that had grown up being told people like him were wrong and broken flared up inside him despite himself, and he realized he was waiting for somebody to tell him he was a disgrace. But all that happened was that Mother's smile got wider. "I should buy you sweets more often. There's kisses in it."

Vasily's heartbeat slowed, and his own smile mirrored Mother's as he relaxed. He'd kissed a man in front of everyone, and nobody cared. It made sense, he supposed. If someone really did have a problem with a man taking up with another man, they'd hardly be lined up for Leo and Felix.

The bodies around them pressed forward and Mother put a protective arm around Vasily as a cheer rang through the crowd. Vasily craned his neck to see, and yes, coming over the rise was the start of the procession. Janus and Thomas, his second-in-command, were sitting ramrod straight on their horses, looking the part in their formal uniforms as they rode past with a slow, measured gait. Two more guards followed, and then there was the flash of sunlight on gold as Leo came into view, smile wide and coronet gleaming, nodding at the crowd. Felix rode alongside, his own coronet glinting in the sun's rays, and while his form on horseback was impeccable, his expression held none of the practiced blandness of Leo's. He kept scrunching up his nose, putting a hand up to his coronet, and tugging at the fastening of his cape. Vasily could have sworn he saw Leo mouth the word *behave*.

They passed at a respectable clip, slowly enough for everyone to get a good look at their king and his husband, who were nodding and smiling as they went. "Ah, aren't they a lovely couple, though?" a woman next to Vasily said with a wistful sigh. "I wish my Jem would look at me like that."

And indeed, Felix was gazing at Leo with unconcealed affection. The corners of his mouth were turned up in a secret smile, and Leo was looking back at him like they were the only two people there and the crowd around them had ceased to exist. In that moment, Vasily understood why Felix was willing to put up with all the pomp and circumstance his new position required.

Mother's arm across his shoulders tightened. "Besotted, they are," he agreed, and the woman gave a nod of approval.

Vasily leaned into Mother's side, enjoying the warmth of him as they watched Davin, the bishop, and the heads of a dozen noble families ride by. The rear of the procession was brought up by Jeremy and another guard, both beaming from ear to ear. Jeremy waved to someone in the crowd and said something, and Vasily caught the shape of the words, "Hi, Mum!"

The crowd fell in behind the procession and followed them down to the harbour, and Vasily and Mother were swept along. Once there, the bishop stood at the top of the path that led to the harbour, facing the fleet of small boats bobbing in the sparkling ocean. He extended one arm as he began to speak, reading from a scroll. He seemed to go on forever, and his sonorous voice combined with the afternoon sun had Vasily blinking in an effort to stay awake.

Mother pressed a kiss to the top of his head and said in an undertone, "Rumour has it he's the reason Felix refused a formal wedding. Said he'd be asleep before he could say I do."

"I'd believe it," Vasily said. Still, he found himself stifling his yawn from habit. Princes didn't yawn in public, no matter how dull the ceremony.

He straightened up and tried to pay attention and was relieved to find that the man had finally pronounced the blessing. If the swell of cheering from the crowd was anything to go by, he wasn't the only one who'd been ready for the bishop to stop talking.

The cheering increased when Leo, Felix, and a smiling Davin stepped up next to the bishop, flanked by Thomas and Janus. All three of them held bulging purses. The crowd thinned as the people hurried to form a queue that snaked all the way around the harbour wall. "It's the royal coin," Mother murmured in response to Vasily's unasked question. "It's meant to be for the fishermen, but everyone joins in, and His Majesty never says no. People all want the luck of the king."

"Do they really believe it brings them luck?"

Mother huffed out a soft laugh. "Well, they're getting a day off and a gold coin. I'd say that's lucky."

They spent some time wandering around the stalls hand in hand, watching the juggler who was meant to be there for the children but who held just as many adults enthralled. Vasily dug in his pockets and found a three-penny bit to slip into the man's hat, the thrill of having money of his own and the choice of how to spend it still fresh, even now.

He dug out another coin at the next vendor and bought them both slices of hot roasted meat wrapped in fresh bread rolls, and after they'd eaten they strolled down the path that led to the ocean.

Vasily stood on the shore, tipping his head back and inhaling lungfuls of sea and salt, the cries of the gulls rending the air. "Are you sure you're not a selkie, lad?" Mother asked. "I've never seen someone enjoy the ocean so much who wasn't born to it."

He laughed and shook his head. "Definitely not a selkie. I do love it, though."

They stayed there, enjoying the soft breeze and the sunlight, and Mother reached out and tangled their fingers together. Vasily felt contentment wash over him. This was everything he'd imagined when he left home, and more besides.

Mother nudged him and nodded towards the steps, where the tail end of the queue was visible. "Are you sure you don't want to go line up? Gold coin and the king's luck?"

Vasily shook his head, smiling. "I don't need the king's luck. I already have you."

If the heated kiss Mother pulled him into was anything to go by, he felt the same.

Vasily just hoped he'd still feel that way when he found out the truth.

Chapter Thirteen

"I can't believe you let me sleep!"

Mother turned upon hearing Vasily's voice, and his heart warmed at the sight of his lover with his hair still sleep-mussed and his shirt untucked. His cheeks were rosy, he was breathing heavily like he'd run the entire way from Mother's cottage, and he was still gorgeous. "You needed the rest."

"But the king and the prince consort will be here any minute for their ride, and I still have to—"

Mother stepped aside to reveal Blackbird and Shadow, both saddled and ready to go. "I did it, lad."

He led the horses out and looped their reins over a post, and Vasily followed. He had that crease in the centre of his brow that appeared whenever he was trying and failing to be annoyed. "It's not your job," he grumbled.

Mother resisted the urge to kiss Vasily's scowl away. "I'm the stablemaster. It's my job if I say it is. Besides," he added, stepping closer and sliding his hands into Vasily's trousers in one smooth motion to tuck the tails of his shirt in, "you looked too pretty sleeping to wake you."

Vasily huffed. "My hair was a bird's nest and I still had your spend on my belly from when we fell asleep last night. Pretty's not the word you're looking for."

"You're right," Mother said, sliding the hand that had been tucking Vasily's shirt in lower and cupping his arse. "I meant to say stunning. Breathtaking. Perfect."

Vasily ducked his head and gave Mother a reluctant smile, looking up from under his lashes, his cheeks pink. "Flattery will get you everywhere."

Mother did so love it when he could make his boy blush just by being sweet. Part of him wondered what Vasily's upbringing had been like that he was so swayed by the slightest sign of affection. But then Vasily cupped Mother's face in his palms and kissed him long and slow, and Mother was distracted from thinking about Vasily's past as he melted into his embrace. No matter how many times they did this, he still couldn't get enough of Vasily—in his arms, in his bed, in his life. The past month had been better than anything he'd ever dreamed of.

The sounds of laughter and footsteps signalled the arrival of the king and the prince consort, and Mother pulled back with a sigh. He walked slowly over to the door—Vasily had fucked him with all the enthusiasm of youth last night, and Mother was still feeling it—and by the time they got outside, Leo and Felix were already astride their horses.

Felix raised an eyebrow at Mother's hitching gait. "I was going to ask how the courting's going, but you look like you've had a right royal rogering."

Vasily tensed next to him.

"Flick, don't," Leo said, narrowing his eyes at his husband.

"What? It's just an expression!" Felix said, eyes wide.

Mother got the feeling he was missing something, but before he could ponder on it, the steady clip-clop of hooves signalled the approach of Thomas riding over from the general stables. "Ready, sires?"

"I still don't see why we need a guard," Felix muttered. "I'm perfectly capable—"

"Of getting shot at, kidnapped, and falling off your horse, sire," Thomas said, "and that was while you *were* the bodyguard." Mother detected a glint of amusement in the man's eyes, but his expression was otherwise implacable.

"Shall we ride?" Leo said brightly, and with a click of his tongue, he encouraged Blackbird towards the gate. Felix followed behind and once they were far enough ahead to give the illusion of privacy, Thomas joined them.

Mother watched them ride away, and whereas once he might have gazed wistfully and wondered if he'd ever have a partner of his own, now he reached out and ran his fingers through Vasily's tangled hair, revelling in the fact that he got to do so. "They'll be a while. Why don't you go and get some sleep?"

"I'm fine," Vasily said, leaning into Mother's touch. He gazed at the retreating figures on horseback. "A king and a groom. Who would have credited it?" he said quietly, something almost wistful in his tone.

"Aye, an odd match but a good one. They're happy as pigs in mud."

Vasily turned to Mother, a smile playing around the edges of his mouth. "Are pigs in mud happy? Did someone ask them?"

Mother laughed. "Nothing happier than a pig in mud." He gave into the urge to press a kiss to Vasily's temple and added, "Except maybe me when I'm with you."

Vasily's breathing hitched and he turned to Mother, eyes wide. "Really?"

Mother's heart clenched, and he was overwhelmed with a wave of affection for this strange, contradictory boy who he was now certain had stolen his heart. He drew him into an embrace and whispered into his ear. "Really, Vas. You're—" How to tell Vasily what he meant, how Mother felt, without scaring him off?

He wanted to chase the uncertainty out of Vasily's gaze once and for all, but his own feelings were so big that he was afraid to burden Vasily with the weight of them.

But when Vasily tilted his head up from where it was resting on Mother's chest, he wore an expression of naked hope. "Yes?"

And how was Mother meant to hold back what he felt in the face of that?

"You're it for me, lad," he said, voice rough with emotion.

Vasily pressed a kiss to his lips. "Me too," he said in the barest of whispers, and anything else he'd been going to say was lost because Mother couldn't contain himself—he had to touch, taste, claim. He backed Vasily up against the side of Blackbird's stall, the wood rough under his palms as he planted his hands on the wall and crowded in close, kissing Vasily like his life depended on it.

Vasily's chest heaved and he opened his mouth to let Mother in, letting out tiny gasps as he grasped at Mother's shirt, clutching fistfuls of fabric and kissing right back, desperate and hungry.

Heat gathered in Mother's gut, the strength of the desire that surged through him catching him by surprise, just as it did every time.

How had he ever lived without this?

"Bryn," Vasily gasped against his mouth. "Can I—" He brought his hands to Mother's chest and pushed him backward, then slid to his knees, fumbling at the lacing of Mother's trousers. His heart thundered in his chest at what Vasily was suggesting.

They were in *public*.

Well, an empty stable. Still, it definitely wasn't somewhere the door could be closed and privacy guaranteed. Vasily gazed up at him, eyes wide and pleading. He looked so pretty, ready and willing there on his knees, that despite their location, Mother's cock stiffened, throbbing with an urgency that refused to be denied.

He turned so his back was against the stall and they were at least hidden from view if anyone were to glance inside the door, and joined Vasily in tugging his trousers down his thighs. His cock sprang free of its confines and slapped against his belly, the tip already slick.

Vasily didn't hesitate, and Mother had to slap a hand across his mouth to hold back the shout that erupted from him when Vasily leaned forward and swallowed his cock. The sudden wet heat and the resulting surge of pleasure had Mother letting out a low groan.

He clutched at Vasily's hair, and Vasily glanced up from under long lashes and smiled around Mother's cock. He slid his mouth farther down the shaft, teasing the length with his tongue in a way that made his nerves tingle and the sensations spiral, twisting and curling, into a single low, blooming thrum of heat deep in his belly that threatened to ignite at any second.

"Vas," Mother panted, unable to stop his hips rocking forward, seeking more. His grip on Vasily's hair tightened, and Vasily let out a pleased groan, his eyes fluttering closed.

Vasily, with his head thrown back, eyes closed, and his face a picture of bliss, was the most beautiful sight Mother had ever seen. Every thought flew out of his head as he rutted forward, lost to everything but the heat of Vasily's mouth, the rasp of his tongue against silken skin, and the coiling want in his gut as Vasily licked and teased. Mother couldn't have stopped the desperate whimpers coming out of his mouth if he'd wanted to.

Vasily chose that moment to slide a hand up the back of Mother's thigh and slip it between his arse cheeks, dragging his thumb over his sensitive hole. The dry rasp was all it took to have Mother's balls drawing up tight and white heat crackling down his spine, tightly coiled need unspooling as pleasure surged through him, sudden and overwhelming. His spine arched, and he grabbed Vasily's head between his palms, holding him in place as he thrust forward one final time, spilling his release.

Vasily swallowed around his pulsing length, the constriction of his throat sending trails of pleasure dancing across Mother's sensitive skin like fireflies lighting up the evening sky. Mother shuddered and loosened his grip in Vasily's hair, running his fingers through the strands as he fought to catch his breath. "Gods alive, lad," he panted out.

Vasily released Mother's softening cock and gazed up at him. His lips were plump and red, his eyes dark with want, and Mother didn't hesitate to drop to his knees beside him and pull him in for a kiss, heedless of the taste of himself that lingered on Vasily's tongue.

With Vasily's body a warm weight against his, Mother was desperate to touch him. He slipped his hands under Vasily's shirt, skating his fingertips over his ribs and tracing his pecs, hungry for more of that warm, smooth skin against his palms.

Vasily groaned at the touch, a needy sound that Mother thought he might never get enough of. He wasted no time dragging Vasily's trousers open and shoving them down, underwear and all. His cock sprang forth, twitching and straining against nothing, the head damp and flushed dark red. Knowing what Vasily liked, Mother licked his palm and wrapped a hand around the shaft, his grip firm. Vasily let out a broken whimper.

Mother didn't tease, instead stroking him in a fast rhythm that had Vasily clutching at Mother's shoulders hard enough that his fingertips turned white. He pushed up into the circle of Mother's fist in a series of short, urgent thrusts before he doubled over, tensing. His cock spurted hard enough that it hit not only his stomach but went halfway up his chest. Mother stroked him through it, gentling his grip when Vasily shuddered and squirmed.

Burying his face in the crook of Mother's neck, Vasily's breath was warm against the skin of his collarbone as he let out a contented hum. Mother eased them down to a sitting position, nuzzling at Vasily's throat and pressing soft kisses to the skin there while Vasily sprawled across his lap. He was aware that his bollocks were hanging out and that he was sitting in the dirt with a piece of straw jabbing him in the arse, but with Vasily lax and pliant in his arms, he found he didn't much care.

He'd get up in a minute or so and find a cloth to wipe Vasily down. Then he'd dust his arse off, and they'd straighten their clothing and get to work.

But for now, he'd take a moment just to enjoy this.

～

Several hours later, their morning frolic was just a fond, distant memory for Mother. It had all been fine, with Leo and Felix returning from their ride and Vasily tending to their horses while Mother supervised the rest of his staff. But then one of the young grooms in the general stables had left a gate open. Before Mother could do anything other than shout a warning, a newly purchased and untrained yearling had bolted without so much as a leading rope. Mother hadn't hesitated to take off after it on horseback before it got away completely.

It had taken him, Vasily, and Ollie an hour to corner the yearling, and it had still been the devil's own job to catch him and get a rope on him. In the end it had been Ollie, with his calm approach and gentle demeanour, who'd managed to slip a halter onto the trembling, wide-eyed horse, making soft, soothing sounds all the while.

It was further proof that Ollie would make an excellent groom, and Mother decided he'd talk to the boy about apprenticing him.

He slid from his horse, hissing between his teeth at the sharp ache in his arse when his boots hit the ground. If he'd known he'd be riding today, he might not have let Vasily plough his arse last night—generally, they'd learned to account for such things.

Although then again, he might have. It always felt so damnably good, and when Vasily flashed his wicked smile, Mother found him impossible to say no to.

He walked his horse back to the yard to find Vasily in the stables, his freshly groomed mount already in her stall. His face lit up when he saw Mother. "I wondered where you'd gotten to. Why didn't you ride back?"

Mother raised an eyebrow, and Vasily tried and failed to keep the satisfied smile off his face. But he also took the reins from Mother and removed his horse's saddle, waving away Mother's offer of help. "You sit. I'll do it."

He wanted to object but his aching muscles won, and Mother sank gratefully onto a low stool and watched as Vasily groomed the horse with long, sweeping arcs of the brush, giving Mother a most pleasant view of the planes of his back flexing under his shirt. Vasily moved expertly, and it didn't take him long to finish the task. He petted the horse's nose and murmured sweet nothings that would have made Mother jealous, if he hadn't had the man in his bed just last night.

Vasily checked the water and bolted the stall before turning to Mother. "This is going to sound terrible," he said, "and I'd never hurt anyone deliberately, but part of me likes that you can feel where I've been the next day." He wrinkled his nose, and a faint blush dusted his cheeks. "Like you're...you're mine."

He was earnest and apologetic all at once, and Mother's stomach swooped pleasantly at the word *mine*.

He strode over to Vasily, wrapping his arms around him and resting their foreheads together. "I *am* yours," he said, his heart full to bursting as it tried to contain the depth of his feelings, "and I always will be, no matter what."

Vasily's breath caught. "No matter what?"

"No matter what," Mother said, and in that moment he meant it utterly.

Vasily's face did something complicated and he stepped

back. "I like you, Mother. More than like you, I think. But there are things you don't know about me."

Mother had a momentary flash of unease, but he took a deep breath and reminded himself that he'd always known that Vasily had secrets. Whatever it was, how bad could it really be?

Vasily was sweet and caring, and so charmingly naïve in so many ways that Mother found it difficult to believe that whatever he was hiding could be anything too terrible.

"It doesn't matter what you tell me. It won't make a difference," he declared.

Vasily bit his lip. "I can assure you, it most definitely will." His voice shook, and he looked so lost, so *resigned*, that Mother desperately wanted to prove him wrong. Whatever it was, he wouldn't *let* it change how he felt.

Not when he'd fallen so utterly for his groom.

"Tell me, Vasily," he said quietly in the same soothing tone he'd use on a spooked horse.

Vasily opened his mouth to speak, then glanced around. "Not here," he said. "I'd like to tell you in private. Can we go to mine?" He had a point. They were alone for now, but there were sounds of activity out in the yard, and Mother knew that any minute now one of his stable boys was bound to come wandering through.

"Of course," Mother said. As they walked through the stable yard, he paused long enough to rattle off a string of instructions to one of his more competent grooms before they made their way to Vasily's cottage.

They went inside and Vasily sat at the small table, his hands twisting around each other and one leg tapping nervously. Mother sat opposite him. When Vasily remained silent, Mother reached out, took one hand, and waited.

"My family—" Vasily broke off, heaving in a great shaky breath. "I don't even know how to say it."

For one terrible moment, Mother was convinced that Vasily's family ran Koroslova's infamous criminal network, the one known for bloodshed and ruthlessness that was only ever mentioned in low whispers in shadowed corners. He dismissed the thought almost immediately because Vasily was made of sunshine and laughter, and the idea of him being involved in anything murderous was preposterous.

Still.

"Your family aren't...they're not the Valnakovs, are they?"

"What? No, of course not!"

"Then what, lad? What's so terrible that you can't tell me?" He gave Vasily's hand a reassuring squeeze.

The click of Vasily's throat as he swallowed was audible. He took a deep breath, straightened his spine, pushed his shoulders back, and declared, "You need to know who I am. My name is Prince Vasily Anatoly Alexei Pasha Petrov, and I am the fourth son of King Alexei and Queen Irina of Koroslova."

His heartbeat thundered in Mother's ears, and he felt all the blood draining from his face, one word standing out among all the others.

Prince?

Prince?

He made a choked sound and pulled his hand back instinctively out of the prince's—*the prince's!*—grasp.

Mother wondered what he was supposed to say or do. Was he supposed to pretend this didn't matter? Of *course* it mattered.

How could it not?

Vasily being a prince changed *everything*. He was part of a world that was far more impressive than anything Mother had to offer, and that meant that whatever was between them could never be more than it was. How could Mother even think he might mean something to Vasily—*Prince* Vasily, he silently corrected—when he was nothing but a stablemaster?

His throat ached with the need to beg for an explanation, to ask why Vasily had lied, but he couldn't get the words out.

"Bryn?" Vasily said, his voice small. The prince was staring at him, his bottom lip quivering as he waited for a response. But Mother had none to give him, because when he looked at Vasily now, he didn't just see the man he was falling—*had* fallen—for.

Vasily was a *prince*, and try as he might, Mother couldn't simply wave a hand and accept the fact that the man who had sucked his cock in the stables this morning might also one day rule an entire kingdom. And since Mother wasn't sure which of them he was addressing, his sweet groom or the prince of Koroslova, he found himself unable to speak at all.

He needed to get away, to think. If he stayed here, if Vasily tried to talk about this while he was still reeling, Mother was sure he'd say something they'd both regret.

In desperation, he fell back on a lifetime of practiced formality. He ducked his head. "Begging your pardon, sire, but I think it's best I go."

And then, ignoring the flash of hurt in Vasily's eyes and pushing aside his own desire to comfort him, Mother walked out the door.

"Wait!"

At the sound of Vasily's voice, Mother stilled despite himself, but when he heard boots crunching on the gravel, he whirled on his heel and held up a palm. Vasily stopped, and Mother forced himself to swallow around the ache of impending loss. He gritted out, "Don't. I need to go. I can't—" He broke off, unsure of what he was trying to say.

Vasily's shoulders slumped and he nodded. His whispered apology was almost too quiet to hear, but Mother heard it anyway.

"I'm...I'm sorry."

Well, that made two of them.

Chapter Fourteen

When Mother halted on the path, Vasily hoped just for a moment that he was coming back. Vasily wanted a chance to explain himself, to reassure Mother that nothing had changed. Then the two of them could come up with some way to stay together, now and in the future.

But Mother made it clear that he didn't want to talk to him, and while Vasily was desperate to follow him, to make him listen, he didn't know what Mother was feeling right now. And maybe it made him a coward, but it was easier to let him walk away, even as his heart ached and his vision blurred with tears.

He watched the path long after Mother had disappeared, at a loss as to what to do with himself. Did he go back to the stables, act like nothing had happened, and bury himself in his work? Or did he hide in his cottage and nurse his heartbreak until something happened to make it better?

Could anything make it better?

He went inside, locked the door, and slumped on the bed, staring at the ceiling. The blankets were still rumpled from last night, and when he buried his face in the pillow, he could smell traces of the scent he associated with Mother—hay and sweat and sex all rolled into one. He inhaled deeply, and a sob caught in his throat.

He hadn't asked to be born a prince, and it wasn't fair that Mother was rejecting him for it. But blaming Mother made his gut churn with wrongness. It wasn't *his* fault that Vasily was a prince either.

And Vasily had hardly delivered the news delicately, had he? Spouting all his names like a schoolboy reciting his lessons or a soldier rattling off his rank as if he was trying to prove he was somehow better than Mother—when the truth of it was, Mother was ten times the man he'd ever be.

Vasily missed him already.

He was blaming Felix, he decided, with all his *tell the truth and you can have a happy ending*. Just because Felix and Leo had been lucky enough to overcome their obstacles, that didn't mean Vasily could. He was just a fourth son from a kingdom where loving another man was unthinkable.

Still, if there was one thing that had been drummed into him over the years, it was that nothing was ever solved by crying about it. He needed to pull himself together before he fell apart completely. He forced himself to sit up, using the heel of his hand to dash away his unshed tears, then stood and splashed his face with the cold water from his washstand.

His stomach clenched, reminding him that he hadn't eaten today.

He ran a hand through his messy hair, twisting it up into a loose bun, and after taking a deep breath, he opened the door and stepped outside. His gaze automatically went to Mother's cottage, but of course the door was firmly closed. With a sigh, Vasily walked up to the castle alone.

He was quiet during his late lunch and barely tasted his meal, too busy running through what had happened in his mind. He could understand that Mother had been shocked, but he'd been stunned and more than a little hurt at the speed with which Mother had rejected him. Vasily had expected surprise, or perhaps even a demand for an explanation. What he hadn't expected was for Mother to walk away without so much as a second glance.

Mother must hate him.

He dropped his spoon into his soup bowl and stood, carrying it over to the sink and washing it himself. Since he was here well past lunchtime, he could hardly expect the kitchen girls to clean up after him, not when they were already busy with dinner preparation.

He wondered if Mother was busy in the stables or if he'd gone somewhere quiet to get over their fight.

Only, it hadn't really been a fight, had it?

Vasily ran through their conversation once more, examining it carefully. He'd told Mother who he was, and Mother had excused himself and left.

Vasily was hit by a desperate longing to seek Mother out. After all, Mother had *said* he was Vasily's—no matter what. Surely that had to count for something.

But then, what if, when Vasily went to him, Mother made it clear he wasn't interested in continuing to court him? What if Mother's *"I can't"* had meant "I can't be with you"?

Vasily wasn't sure if his heart could take being rejected twice in a day.

He stuffed his hands in his pockets and walked dejectedly back to his cottage, but when he got there, he stopped with his hand on the doorknob, unable to take the thought of sitting inside with nothing but his thoughts for company.

He turned and walked back up to the castle, letting his feet lead him to the training yard, drawn by the steady thud of boots and the clash of staffs. When he turned the corner of the castle, he was greeted by the sight of the captain of the guard sprawled on his arse in the dirt with a young man standing over him, wearing a stricken expression. "Sorry, Captain! I didn't mean it!" the boy babbled, hastily offering Janus a hand.

Janus waved him off, standing with a fluid grace that belied his years. "What are you sorry for, Seth?"

"You're the captain! And I just knocked you down!" The boy's eyes were as wide as saucers.

Janus laughed. "I'm supposed to be teaching you to fight. If you've managed to put me on my arse, I've done it right." He clapped a hand on Seth's shoulder and looked over at the rest of the young men. "Anyone else want to try their luck?"

"I will," Vasily found himself saying as he stepped forward.

The captain raised an eyebrow in silent enquiry, and when Vasily jutted his chin out and nodded, Janus picked up a staff and threw it at him. Vasily caught it deftly. He wasn't an expert by any means, but his father had always insisted his sons be able to defend themselves, so Vasily could hold his own well enough if he had to. And losing himself in the to and fro of a mock battle might be just the thing to distract himself from his thoughts.

They circled each other, Vasily keeping his stance wide and low and his guard up. Janus might be older, but his years of experience meant he was a skilled fighter. A few weeks ago, Vasily had watched him drop a man twice his size with a well-placed blow.

Janus darted forward, his weapon swinging, and Vasily ducked back, lifting his staff to stop the blow. It was enough of a threat to have his heart racing, even though he wasn't in any real danger. He stopped thinking about Mother and instead focused on finding an opportunity to land a blow of his own.

His staff bounced off Janus's shoulder, and the man muttered "Whoreson" under his breath, clutching the site of the blow and grimacing. Vasily made the mistake of letting his attention stray, worried he'd done more damage than intended, and Janus was quick to take advantage. He drove forward with a flurry of blows that had Vasily bending backward with his staff extended as he fought them off.

It was while he was unbalanced that Janus kicked the legs right out from under him, and he landed with a solid thump that sent a rattle all the way up his spine. Janus grinned down at him, teeth gleaming. "Again?"

"Again," Vasily said. He was short of breath, his arse throbbed in a way that told him it would bruise, and he was fairly certain the new recruits were laughing at him, but it was still preferable to sitting around thinking about the way Mother had walked out on him.

The next round ended up much the same as the first one, with him in the dirt. But by the third go-round, all Vasily's hard-learned lessons started to come back to him, and there were several times when he *almost* got the upper hand. He dared to think he might even win this one—right before Janus surged forward and overpowered him in a single bold move that had Vasily flat on his back, his staff knocked from his grip and his hands pinned over his head. He wondered if he'd ever really had a chance.

"That's enough," Janus said, panting and ruddy-faced. "Time to let the young bucks have a turn."

Vasily, whose own chest was heaving like a bellows, grinned. "Oh, I don't know. I could go another—"

Janus had him flipped onto his front with his arms pulled halfway up his back before he could finish the sentence, and his voice was low as he growled in Vasily's ear. "We're done. Let an old man rest."

It was when he let go and Vasily rolled over that he noticed that Janus's breathing was still coming in unsteady rasps, and his hairline was stained dark with sweat beading at his temples. "Of course," he said, getting to his feet and grimacing when he patted at his tender rump to dislodge the dirt there.

Janus stood, resting his elbows on one of the rails

surrounding the training ring. "Well, come on then!" he barked at his recruits. "Pair up, the lot of you, and show me what you've learned!"

The young men were quick to pair up before stepping into the dirt circle and starting to spar, and under the cover of their clattering staffs and the occasional curse, Janus said quietly, "You told Mother who you are, then?"

Vasily swallowed. "How did you know?" Just thinking about Mother had his stomach tying itself in knots all over again.

Janus shrugged. "Figured you wouldn't be slinking around the castle in the middle of the day otherwise. I take it he didn't react well?"

Leaning on the railing next to Janus, Vasily let his head sink down between his arms and stared at the dirt, squeezing his eyes shut against the sudden stinging there. "He hates me."

Janus sighed. "Did he say that?"

"No," Vasily said. "He didn't need to. He walked away."

A calloused hand landed on the nape of Vasily's neck, warm and reassuring. "Don't be so quick to assume. That was quite some news you gave him. Knowing Mother, he's gone off to think about it, that's all. Don't give up hope."

"Do you think so?" Vasily turned his head to find Janus watching him, mouth curved up in a sympathetic smile.

"I think Mother is a man who, for the first time in his life, has found someone he's head over heels for. And now he's found out that person isn't who he thought they were. Do you blame him for needing some time to get used to the idea? What if you suddenly found out he was the ninth Earl of Evergreen?"

Vasily blinked and propped himself up as he considered how he'd react to finding out Mother was someone other than he claimed. "That...makes sense," he said slowly, and a spark of hope ignited in his chest. "So, you don't think he hates me?"

Janus raised his eyebrows. "Vasily, that man adores you.

Knowing him, it's more likely he thinks he's not good enough for you."

The very idea that Mother might think that had Vasily scowling. "Bryn is far better than I deserve."

Janus's eyebrows inched higher. "He told you his *other* name?" He shook his head and chuckled. "If you ever needed any more proof that he's gone on you, that's it right there. Exactly four people know that name outside of his parents."

The spark of hope flickered into a tiny flame, and the pressure in Vasily's chest eased the slightest bit. "So...what should I do?" he asked.

"You wait. When he's ready to talk, he'll find you. Then you listen to what he has to say, and with any luck you'll work out what happens next. It might not be easy, though. You *are* still a prince."

Vasily didn't want to admit it, not when there was a chance that Mother didn't hate him after all, but he knew that Janus was right. Still, he had more hope now than he'd had an hour ago. "You're a wise man, Captain."

Janus grinned. "I just know Mother Jones." He looked past Vasily's shoulder then and shouted, "Aubrey! Watch your footing! He'll have you over in a—" There was a dull thud followed by a startled squawk and laughter from the rest of the recruits. Janus ran a hand down his face in a timeless gesture of defeat and muttered, "I'm getting too old for this."

"Thank you," Vasily said. He still didn't feel anything close to good about what had happened, but he didn't feel quite as devastated as he had before either.

Janus gave a nod, then hauled himself upright and walked across the yard, and the last thing Vasily heard as he walked away was Janus telling his recruits to pair up and try again.

It was later than he'd realised, and he ended up going to the stables. At the end of the day, he had a job to do, and it wasn't like Blackbird or Shadow cared about whether he and Mother were on the outs or not. They just wanted to be fed.

Mother was nowhere to be seen. He wasn't at dinner either, and the windows in his cottage were still dark when Vasily checked. He was miserable with no company, so Vasily climbed into bed—alone—for the first time in almost a month.

It was a long time before he fell asleep.

~

The next morning Mother didn't come and join him for breakfast.

All Vasily's doubts and fears that Mother hated him came rushing back, along with a new, added worry that perhaps Mother had gone and gotten drunk on cider, fallen into the ocean, and drowned. He pushed the thought aside, aware that he was being dramatic. For one thing, unlike Vasily, Mother knew how to swim.

Still, Mother's absence ached like the empty socket of a tooth, a space that refused to remain unnoticed—which was ridiculous. It had been less than a day. But nonetheless, Vasily found himself hurrying down to the stables, convinced that Mother would be there barking orders at his grooms and whispering soft words to his horses, just like always.

Except he wasn't.

Instead, it was the prince consort who he found feeding Blackbird half a carrot. Felix was wearing a ratty shirt, a stained pair of trousers, and old boots, and Vasily wondered at his attire. He didn't look like he was here to ride.

"Sire?"

Felix swung around to face him. "Vasily! I hope you don't mind, but Leo has those quarterly meetings, and I'd sooner poke myself in the eye with a sharp stick than sit through those, so I thought I'd hide out here and run the stables. You can have the day off."

Vasily blinked. "Pardon?"

Felix arched an eyebrow at him. "I'll take care of the horses, Vasily."

"But..." Vasily twisted the end of his ponytail around his fingertips.

Felix folded his arms across his chest. "As prince consort, I'm telling you to take the day off. It isn't a suggestion."

He raised his eyebrows. "Are you actually trying to use your royal position to tell me what to do?"

Felix grinned. "I've never done it before. I wanted to try it, just once."

Vasily felt a smile forming in spite of himself before he remembered that he was blaming Felix for this whole mess. "I'm not actually your subject. You do know that?"

Felix's expression softened. "I heard it didn't go well with Mother, and I thought you might need a break, that's all. And I won't lie, I miss my horses. So do us both a favour and take the day?"

Blackbird snorted as if in agreement, and Felix pressed a kiss to the side of her nose. The easy affection between horse and rider was obvious, and Vasily relented. It wasn't like Mother was here to talk to anyway.

"Fine. I'm going."

"Good man," Felix said. "And Vasily? I wouldn't worry. Mother looks at you like you hung the moon. He'll come around."

"Your father said the same thing."

"Well, then you should trust us both." Felix picked up a water bucket and made a shooing motion with the other hand. "Now get out of here and let me enjoy my day."

Vasily did as he was told.

T he weather was warm with occasional tendrils of a cool breeze, and while Vasily was tempted to hang about his cottage in case Mother came calling, he knew that sitting alone with his thoughts would just make him more anxious with every minute Mother didn't turn up. No, he decided. He'd make the most of the nice weather and go down to the water. Watching the ocean always soothed him.

He meandered down the path towards the docks, along the narrow, cobbled street and past the fishmongers. He went all the way down to the square and along the narrow track that took him to the water's edge, and on impulse slipped his boots off, tying the laces in a knot and slinging them around his neck. He rolled the legs of his trousers up to his knees and dipped one tentative toe in the water.

The shock of the cold took his breath away, and he let out a squawk that blended in perfectly with the cries of the seagulls who circled overhead. He pulled his leg up and out of the water —which proved pointless when a small wave lapped at the toes of his other foot.

He hissed in shock but found that when a second, slightly larger wave washed over his foot, the chill wasn't quite as terrible. He took one careful step forward and then another, until he was calf deep. The cold water was invigorating, and he closed his eyes and let the ocean wash over him as he inhaled the salt air. The coarse sand beneath the soles of his feet shifted whenever he wiggled his toes, and standing there soaking up the sunshine, he felt the tension of the previous day fading, carried away on the sea breeze.

He would have liked to stay in the water longer, but he was uncomfortably aware of the cold seeping into his bones. He opened his eyes and splashed his way to shore before his feet went completely numb. Standing on the beach, he realised that he hadn't thought this through. His feet were wet, and now he couldn't put his boots back on until they'd dried.

He stood there for a moment before deciding that it wasn't really a problem. He walked the length of the beach and up the incline, then along the path that led to the side of the port where the fishing boats unloaded. Habit led him towards the raised section of harbour wall where he and Mother always sat to watch the sunset.

He was hit by a pang of loneliness as he settled himself on the ledge. He missed Mother's customary "Careful, lad," and steadying hand, even though he didn't really need either of them.

He sat, setting his boots down next to him, and swung his legs idly as he took in the view. Sunlight reflected off the surface of the water, the ripples and waves making the light dance in endless patterns. Vasily wasn't sure how long he sat there, but it was long enough that he entered something like a trance, absorbed in the sights and sounds of the tide rolling in, the birds swooping through the air, and the water lapping at the wall as it crept higher, staining the stones dark and claiming them.

A warm hand settled on his shoulder, and his heart soared at the familiar touch. Even without turning, he knew who it was.

"Thought I might find you here," Mother said quietly, easing down to sit next to him and wrapping his arm round Vasily's shoulders, pulling him close. "I'm so sorry, lad."

A lump lodged in Vasily's throat. He turned so he could see Mother's face. "Are you still angry with me?"

"Angry? No, lad. It was a shock, that's all. I needed time to think." He bumped his shoulder against Vasily's.

The affectionate gesture had Vasily's eyes burning. Mother didn't hate him after all. "Where did you go last night?" he asked. "I waited for you."

Mother ducked his head. "I went to the pub. I thought

maybe a pint of ale might help me get over the fact I've been courting a *prince*."

"And did it?"

Mother's mouth twisted in a wry grin. "Aye. And so did the second and third and fourth. The fifth and sixth were a mistake, though. Ended up so soused that I fell asleep under the table and the barkeep put me to bed in the back room." He wrinkled his nose. "Probably explains why I smell like a brewery."

At the thought of Mother's long frame curled up under one of the tables at the pub, Vasily was torn between laughter and relief. "How did you know to find me here?"

"When I woke up, I went to the castle to find you, but Felix said he'd given you the day off. I hoped you'd be here since, well. It's our place, isn't it?"

Our place.

That didn't sound like something somebody would say if they were planning to end a courtship, and Vasily felt a flicker of hope, followed by the urge to explain. "I'm sorry," he said hoarsely. "I had permission from my parents to travel for a year. Not as a prince, just as Vasily. And it was wonderful, and I felt so *free*." He swallowed and gazed at his lap. "But then I met you, and you were everything I never knew I wanted, and I was afraid to say anything in case I lost you. I know I should have told you. But I just wanted…"

"Shhh, lad. I know. You wanted to be yourself, not a prince," Mother said, turning and tucking one leg under himself so they were facing. There were dark circles under his eyes like he hadn't slept, his hair was a mess, and he was still the most wonderful sight Vasily had ever seen—because he was *here*.

Vasily swallowed thickly. "Now that you know, are we—do you still want—" He couldn't quite get the words out.

Somehow, Mother understood anyway. He caught Vasily's gaze, his eyes filled with warmth and affection. "Yes," he said quietly. "I still want."

The tightness in Vasily's chest eased, and it felt like he could draw breath again. "Are you sure? It doesn't matter that I'm a prince?"

"Course it bloody matters," Mother said, reaching out and clasping Vasily's hand between his palms. "You're fourth in line for the throne, lad."

"Fifth," Vasily corrected. "My brother has a son, so that means—"

Mother raised an eyebrow. "Whether you're fourth or fifth, you're a prince of the realm and I'm the son of a fisherman. I'm sure that someone, somewhere, is going to have a conniption about this. But I've had time to think, and you being a prince doesn't change the fact that I—" He swallowed, then squared his shoulders and declared, "I've gone and fallen in love with you."

Vasily stared, the words echoing around in his skull before he finally made sense of them. "You...love me?"

Mother gave him an uncertain smile. "Sorry, lad. Prince or not, I can't help it. And I know I'm only the stablemaster and not nearly good enough for you, and I don't know how this can work, but the heart wants what it wants. And what I want is to keep you."

The lump in Vasily's throat dissolved into a laugh that bubbled out of his chest, and he felt as light and free as one of the birds who swooped and soared overhead. "You too," he said, breathless. "Love you. I do, I mean." He stopped to catch his breath and tried again, dizzy with relief and exhilaration. "I'm in love with you, Bryn."

Mother's eyes lit up, and his face split in a wide smile. "Oh, thank the gods." he breathed out. He clambered to his feet and extended a hand to pull Vasily up.

Vasily scrambled to stand, and when Mother leaned in for a kiss, he responded eagerly, still overwhelmed. Closing his eyes, he lost himself in the familiar taste of Mother's mouth, a single thought echoing in his head.

Mother *loved* him.

He pulled back long enough to test the shape of it. "You love me, Bryn Jones."

"I love you, Vasily Anatoly Alexei Pasha Petrov," Mother said, grinning, and Vasily wondered how long he'd practiced just to get all the names right.

The corners of Mother's eyes were creased with mirth, his smile wide enough that his crooked tooth peeked out. He was beautiful, and Vasily drank in the sight of him. Just knowing Bryn loved him, he could die right now a happy man.

He took a half step back just so he could see him better.

Except he'd forgotten that he was barefoot, and he found himself slipping on the rounded cobbles at the top of the wall. His legs slid out from under him, sending him backward—and then he was falling, and there was only air beneath him. The sound of it whooshing past drowned out his screams as his hands clutched desperately at nothing.

He had barely a second to think that at least the sea would make for a soft landing before he hit the solid surface with a smack. Pain radiated along his spine and all his limbs as he sank into the water, and between that and the shock of the cold water, all the air left his lungs in a whoosh as bubbles flew around his face. He managed to flail his way to the surface and heaved in a sharp breath, fighting to stay afloat.

Mother's horrified face stared down at him and Vasily tried to call out, but before he could, a wave caught him and smacked him up into the rock wall, and everything went fuzzy round the edges as he sank like a stone.

Chapter Fifteen

Mother froze, blood pounding in his ears as terror washed over him. He watched on, helpless, as Vasily tumbled towards the water. When his body struck the surface with a wet slap, Mother flinched instinctively at the imagined sting of it. Then a wave picked up Vasily and swept him into the rock wall. He went limp, and Mother's heart leapt into his throat.

It was the sight of his body disappearing beneath the surface that spurred Mother to action. He knew the sensible thing would be to run down to the dock and take one of the smaller rowboats out, but there was no *time*. The harbour wasn't overly deep, but Vasily couldn't swim a stroke. By the time Mother got there, Vasily would have been claimed by the depths, and he couldn't let that happen.

Sensible be buggered.

Without a second thought, he pulled off his boots, coat, and shirt, took a deep breath, and dived off the wall.

The water was shockingly cold, stealing his breath, and it took him a moment to find his way back to the surface, blinking and kicking frantically against the pull of the tide. He looked around desperately, but there was no sign of Vasily. He blinked until his vision cleared as he resisted the urge to scream Vasily's name and forced himself to think. He swam closer to the rock wall where he'd last seen him, praying to any god that was listening.

Please. I can't lose him.

Taking a deep breath, he dived under the surface and started searching, muted panic making his heart thud as he surged forward. He glanced over to the left when a flash of colour and movement caught his eye.

Sunlight pierced the water, making Vasily's hair shine like gold as it swayed with the motion of the waves, strands floating over his face while his body drifted lower.

Mother's eyes stung with more than the salt of the ocean, and he surged forward and grabbed desperately at Vasily's shirt. Relief and panic fought for space in his chest as he dragged Vasily close, wrapped an arm around his limp body from behind, and used his remaining breath to fight his way back to the surface.

Vasily was a solid weight in his arms, and it took everything in Mother's power to drag him upward. His lungs burned with the need for air, but he ignored it, concentrating on hauling the body through the water. He struggled against the pull of the waves with every fibre of his being as the sea tried to steal Vasily back.

He kept one arm locked around Vasily's chest and pulled himself upward with the other, praying that his efforts weren't in vain. When he finally broke the surface, he wanted to sob with relief, but he was too busy gasping in great lungfuls of air.

Vasily lay still and quiet in his arms, and for one endless, awful moment, Mother worried that he was too late. But then Vasily dragged in a loud, rasping breath, coughing and sputtering and thrashing instinctively against Mother's hold. Mother tightened his grip, and after a few more seconds of useless struggling, Vasily went limp in his arms. Now, though, the rise and fall of his chest reassured Mother that at least he wasn't carrying a *dead* weight.

Something like a sob clawed its way out of his throat, an ugly, desperate sound, before Mother pushed the swell of emotion down. They weren't out of danger yet. He could fall apart later, once Vasily was safe—but for now, he needed to bloody well *swim*.

He didn't waste time, flipping to his back with a grunt and kicking with as much vigour as he could muster. He concentrated on steering them away from the wall and out towards the end of the rock groyne that separated the harbour from the bay, with its safer, shallower waters and the sandy stretch of beach where Vasily liked to walk.

Mother's chest burned and his arms ached, and for every foot he swam, the waves seemed to drag him back two, but with grim determination he kept going, Vasily clutched against his chest.

Mother could see red oozing from Vasily's temple and staining the strands of his hair pink, in stark relief against his too-pale skin.

He thought of his brother, of the pain of losing him, and kicked harder.

He couldn't go through that twice.

It was as he approached the end of the groyne, chest heaving, that there was the clatter of oars and a shout of, "Oi! Over here!"

Mother turned his head, sputtering at the mouthful of salt water the movement earned him, and saw a rowboat approaching. A young man was at the oars, and Magnus, one of his father's fishing friends, was crouched near the side of the boat with his arms outstretched, ready to haul them aboard.

Mother had never been so happy to see anyone in his life.

He kicked just enough to keep them in one spot, waiting until the rower had positioned the boat as close as they could get without clocking him with the oars. Then he swam them closer, and between Mother pushing and Magnus pulling Vasily by his arms, they got him into the boat, where he landed in a messy sprawl.

Mother hauled himself on board and, heart in his throat, he whispered desperately in Vasily's ear. "Vas? You're safe, love. Come on, wake up."

Vasily lay motionless for a second, and Mother felt a cold prickle of fear creep up his spine. "Come on," he muttered under his breath. He rolled Vasily onto his side and thumped his back before tilting his head. Vasily remained still for a moment longer before his eyes snapped open and, gasping and choking, he lurched upright, clutched at the side of the boat, and promptly vomited over the edge. As he heaved and retched, Mother couldn't fight the relieved grin on his face.

Vasily losing his breakfast was a *good* sign.

"There's a lad!" Magnus said. "Get it out!"

Vasily heaved again, then took several short, rattling breaths.

Mother wrapped an arm around Vasily's shoulders and felt a shiver run through him. "Blankets?" Mother barked, ignoring the way his own soaked trousers clung to his skin like a cold, unwelcome hand running up his thigh, pulling away with a wet, sucking sound every time he moved.

Magnus passed over a grey wool blanket that smelled of fish, and Mother drew it around Vasily's shoulders and pulled him onto the long plank that served as a seat next to him. Vasily gave a miserable burp and spat out another mouthful of bile before he slumped against Mother, his eyes closed.

His breathing was still ragged, but he *was* breathing, and that was the main thing.

Mother wrapped an arm around Vasily's shoulders and wondered if he could have that breakdown now.

He knew better, though. His own breathing was laboured, his muscles burned, and he was still shaking from his rescue efforts, but he wasn't done yet. He had to get Vasily to land and then to the castle and the infirmary, to make sure he really was fine. Mother knew better than most the risks of a near drowning.

A sob caught in his throat.

Vasily had almost *died*.

A hand clapped him on the shoulder, and he looked up to find Magnus perched on the opposite seat, giving him a knowing look. "Love?" he said quietly.

Mother let out a damp laugh. "That obvious, is it?"

Magnus smiled. "No, Mother. You *called* him love."

Mother blinked through his blurred vision. He hadn't even realized, but looking at Vasily's head resting against his chest, he couldn't think of a name that fitted better. "Aye," he said softly. "I reckon I've fallen for him."

"About time you found someone," Magnus said. He reached out and ruffled Mother's hair just like he had when Mother was still a boy, and he was too tired and overwhelmed to take offence.

Instead he gave a nod. "Appreciate you coming out. He's a heavy bugger, this one."

"Guessed you'd need a hand. Brave thing you did, diving in," Magnus said. "Stupid, mind you."

"Wasn't going to let the bastard sea take someone else from me," Mother said roughly.

"Aye," Magnus said quietly, eyes dark with understanding. He'd been the one to deliver the news about his brother, Mother remembered. Perhaps that was why he'd been so quick to row out and help them.

Vasily stirred against his chest, and Mother frowned when he saw that the wound on his head was still bleeding, albeit sluggishly. On closer inspection it looked more like a graze than a cut, and Mother's gut unclenched a little. Still, he ran a hand through Vasily's hair, checking for any hidden injuries. Vasily whined, twisting his head to free himself and burying his face against Mother's collarbone.

"Shhh," Mother said. The boat rose and fell, much more sharply than the low swell they'd been experiencing so far, and Mother glanced up to find they were approaching the shallows. As soon as they were close enough to shore, Magnus vaulted over the side and dragged the boat up the sand, and Mother stood, guiding Vasily to the side. They stepped into the two-inch surf. As they made their way onto the beach, Vasily staggered. Mother steadied him with a hand against his hip and pressed a kiss to his temple, uncaring of the onlookers gathered on the shore. "Let's get you to the infirmary."

"I don't think I can," Vasily said, and promptly passed out.

Mother managed to catch him before he hit the ground, lowering him carefully onto the sand. When he looked up, a man who looked vaguely familiar was standing there with a set of reins in his hand. "Take my horse."

Mother didn't bother trying to put a name to the face. Instead, he nodded his thanks. "Help me lift him?"

Together they slung a still-unconscious Vasily across the front of the horse, and Mother settled behind him and rode towards the castle. The horse was biddable and steady, and it wasn't long before they were riding through the castle gates. Mother slid off the saddle, careful not to dislodge Vasily's prone form, and bellowed at the top of his lungs. *"I need the maester!"*

Three guards came running, Janus and Thomas among them. "Damn it," Janus muttered. "What happened?"

"Fell in the drink. Can't swim," Mother said tersely.

"Thomas," Janus barked, his brow creased with worry.

The guard nodded, scooping Vasily into his arms like he weighed nothing and carrying him inside, Mother and Janus following. "How bad is it?" Janus asked in an undertone.

"I don't know," Mother said. "He's breathing, but he cracked his head on the rocks."

When they reached the infirmary, Janus rapped sharply on the door and pushed inside without waiting for a reply. Thomas deposited Vasily on the bed, and upon catching sight of him, Maester Owens hurried over.

"He near drowned and banged his head," Mother said before the man could ask.

Maester Owens pulled back Vasily's eyelids and peered at him. "Hmmm. Outside, all of you."

"But—"

"Out. Side," the man said, a steely glint in his eye that told Mother there was no point arguing.

Janus hooked his elbow and led him out the door. He nodded at Thomas. "Go and inform His Majesty what's happened." Thomas took off in a long, loping run, and Janus led Mother into a small room next to the infirmary and guided him into a chair. He crouched in front of Mother, his eyes full of compassion. "He's in good hands, Bryn."

It was the use of his name that had Mother falling apart.

All the emotions he'd been struggling to keep at bay came bubbling to the surface, and he found himself awash in fear and anger and worry, all churning together under his skin until he was mad with it, and all he could do was cover his face with his hands and let out hoarse, ugly sobs.

Janus stood, dragging Mother to his feet and wrapping his arms around him, his body a solid, comforting wall for him to lean on as he cried like he hadn't in years, unable to hold back.

Part of it, he knew, was the aftermath of diving into the harbour. But mostly it was that he'd finally, after all these years, found the one person perfect for him, and then he'd almost lost him.

He still might.

As if reading his mind, Janus murmured, "Don't bury your boy yet, Mother. The maester knows what he's doing. Don't I trust him with my own son?"

Mother's breathing hitched, but Janus was right. And, he thought absently, the maester had only made his trademark "hmmm" noise. He hadn't made that horrible hissing-through-his-teeth sound that meant things were really bad.

Maybe Vasily would be all right after all. He gave a shaky sigh and straightened up, scrubbing his hands down his face. "You're far too sensible," he grumbled to hide his embarrassment.

Janus patted his shoulder. "One of us has to be since you're obviously lovestruck." His brows pinched together. "You're freezing."

Mother shrugged. He hadn't noticed.

"You should go and get some dry clothes."

He shook his head, even though now Janus mentioned it, his skin was pebbled with the cold and his bare feet curled in discomfort on the stone floor. "I need to—"

"You need to get dry and warm and then you can come back," came a voice from the corridor. King Leopold arched an eyebrow in a way that left Mother in no doubt that he meant it, but then he looked at Mother properly, doubtless taking in his tear-stained face, and his expression softened. "But first, shall I go in and find out how he is?"

"The maester sent everyone out, sire," Mother said, his heart twisting with worry once again.

Leo snorted. "He won't send *me* out."

And sure enough, Leo pushed the door open, and Mother heard, "Who in damnation—*sire!* My apologies!" before the door closed again.

Janus smirked. "Leo enjoys doing that far too much."

Mother gave a shaky laugh, and while they waited, he found a pile of folded linen squares and blew his nose and wiped his face. It made him feel a little more respectable, at least. He shivered and wrapped his arms around himself.

It wasn't long before the door to the infirmary opened, and Leo emerged. "He's going to be fine," he said before Mother had a chance to ask. "He woke up, just for a few minutes, and the maester says the bump on his head looks worse than it is."

Mother sagged with relief as all the tension left him. "Can I—"

"Once you're dressed and dry," Leo said firmly. "Then you can come back." He paused. "I'll be sending someone to tell Vasily's parents that he's been injured. It's the proper thing, given his position. Vasily was sent here with the intention that he be kept safe, and not to inform the Koroslovan royal family of something like this could spark a diplomatic incident."

Leo watched him carefully as he spoke, as if he expected Mother to disagree, but Mother nodded. "Of course, sire. Vasily's a prince, after all." The words still sounded odd to his own ears, but Mother supposed that would pass with time. Besides, after nearly losing him, Mother was determined that he wasn't going to let Vasily's position come between them. "Get one of the lads to saddle up Archer, sire. He's the fastest ride we've got, and I assume you'll want word to get through as quickly as you can."

"Quite. I'll send Janus. A message like this needs a person with some standing to deliver it." Leo gave him a soft smile, and Mother couldn't help but feel he'd passed some sort of test.

Then Leo shooed Mother towards the door and he didn't even think of arguing. Still barefoot, he made his way to his cottage and hastily stoked the fire, setting a pan of water to heat while he peeled out of his wet trousers and dried his hair. By the time he'd done that, the water had heated, so he washed himself, removing the traces of ocean salt and chasing away the chill at the same time.

He dressed in clean, dry clothes and ran his fingers through his hair, then pulled on his spare boots, anticipation and relief tangled together as he hastened back to the infirmary.

The maester had said Vasily was going to be fine, and that was well and good, but Mother was still shaken by how close he'd come to losing him. He didn't plan on leaving his side anytime soon.

When he arrived back at the infirmary, he knocked softly on the door and Maester Owens let him in. A chair had been set next to the bed. "His Majesty said you'd want to stay," the maester murmured.

"Aye," Mother said. He sat down and reached out, covering Vasily's hand with his own. "Is he really going to be fine?" he asked quietly.

"Thanks to you," the maester said. "I'll leave you alone."

He left, and Mother let himself really look at Vasily. He'd been stripped out of his wet clothes and dressed in a nightshirt, and he looked pale and fragile against the bed linens, with dark circles under his eyes. But the wound on his head had been dressed, and his chest was rising and falling in a reassuring, steady rhythm.

Mother stroked the back of Vasily's fingers, but it wasn't enough. He'd nearly lost the person he loved, and now he needed to be close.

Slipping his boots off, he eased onto the bed behind Vasily and wrapped an arm around him. Vasily nestled back against him and made a contented noise, and the familiarity of it immediately made Mother feel better.

Mother's entire body was a catalogue of aches and pains, and a wave of exhaustion swept over him as he sagged into the mattress like a puppet whose strings had been cut. Still, he found himself smiling because he had Vasily in his arms, and what could be better than that?

Secure in the knowledge that his lover was safe, Mother slept.

Chapter Sixteen

Vasily woke in an unfamiliar bedroom, blinking slowly. His eyes stung, the taste of seawater lingered in his throat, and it felt like one of his horses had kicked him in the head. When he raised a hand to the throbbing spot on his temple, he found a dressing there, and he noted that he was in a nightshirt. It was obviously evening, with the curtains drawn, the fireplace lit, and the room suffused with dim lamplight. A vague scent of herbs permeated the room.

The infirmary, then.

Mother was curled up behind him, one hand resting on Vasily's hip as he let out soft snores, and his presence had memories flooding back.

He let out a shaky breath as remembered panic coursed through him. He recalled the split second of terror and disbelief when his feet had skidded out from under him and sent him plummeting, and the pain of his skull bouncing off the rocks when the waves had dashed him against the wall.

When he'd hit his head, he'd been too dazed to try and stay afloat, and as he'd started to sink, he'd genuinely thought he was going to die. Panic had flooded him as everything had started to go dark, and he'd had to fight the urge to open his mouth, desperate for breath. But then, impossibly, Mother had appeared out of nowhere, a grimly determined rescuing angel, and hauled him to the surface.

Mother had saved him.

The knowledge of how close he'd come to drowning filled him with a sudden, desperate need to be held, and he put his hand on top of the one resting on his hip and drew it around himself, encasing himself in Mother's warmth. The arm tightened as Mother stirred, and his breath was a light breeze against Vasily's ear as he murmured, "All right, love?"

"Want to hold you," Vasily mumbled, turning in Mother's arms and burying his face against his chest as his heart hammered. The fabric of Mother's shirt was rough against his cheek, but underneath it his heartbeat was steady and strong, just like Mother himself. The familiar rhythm along with Mother's presence worked to soothe him, until he felt a little less off-kilter and his heart stopped racing quite so much. "I was so afraid," he admitted.

Mother kissed the top of his head and pulled him closer. "You're not the only one. Thought I'd lost you for a minute there." His voice was unsteady, and he reached out and brushed Vasily's hair away from his face. "Couldn't see a bloody thing underwater." He twirled one of Vasily's locks idly around a finger. "This was what saved you. Shone like gold, it did."

Vasily propped himself on one elbow and looked down to find Mother watching him, his expression a mixture of devotion and possessiveness that warmed Vasily inside and chased away some of the lingering terror. He leaned forward and pressed a kiss to Mother's cheek. "Thank you," he whispered, "for diving in after me."

"I'll always dive in, if it's you," Mother said, his gaze intense.

Vasily didn't doubt for a moment that he meant it, and the words settled something inside of him. He decided he'd spent long enough thinking about his close call when really, the most important event of the day had been Mother's declaration as they'd sat on the harbour wall. "You said you loved me. You even used all my names."

"I do love you," Mother said, a smile curling up the corners of his mouth, and he looked so pleased with himself that Vasily couldn't resist leaning in and kissing him—a soft, tiny thing but thrilling all the same because he was alive to do it.

"I love you too," he said when he pulled away. It suddenly seemed important that he not miss a single chance to say it.

Mother's expression turned soft, and he cupped Vasily's face with one broad palm and guided him close, then kissed him with a quiet passion, gentle but persistent. Parting his lips, Vasily welcomed Mother in, mapping the inside of his mouth with equal fervour. Mother fitted against Vasily like they'd been made for each other, and kissing him was like coming home. They stayed like that, kissing soft and slow, until a knock at the door interrupted them.

Vasily rolled back onto the bed, wincing at the pull in his muscles, while Mother went and opened the door.

Maester Owens bustled in, making a pleased noise when he saw Vasily sitting up. "You're awake! Excellent. Mr. Jones was supposed to come and get me," he said, shooting Mother a narrow look.

Mother ignored him.

The maester turned to Vasily, pulling out a wooden cylinder and pressing it to his chest. "Deep breaths in and out," he ordered. Vasily did as he was told, and the maester put his ear to the other end of the tube. After several breaths he nodded and moved the tube to his back, saying, "Again." When he lifted his head, his smile was more of a relief than Vasily wanted to admit. "Your lungs sound clear. You took a knock to the head, and you've got some scrapes, but there are no serious injuries."

"So I can go home?" Vasily asked.

The maester hesitated. "I'd prefer it if you weren't alone."

Vasily glanced across at Mother, who was sitting in the chair at the side of the bed. He gave a tiny nod. "I can stay with him."

The maester sighed. "Fine. Vasily can go home if you keep an eye on him. But he's not to exert himself in *any* way. No strenuous activities for at least three days."

Mother affected an innocent look. "So, no working with the horses, you mean?"

Maester Owens raised an eyebrow. "You know *exactly* what activities I'm talking about, Mr. Jones."

Mother's ears turned pink.

Vasily swallowed his disappointment. He found himself craving Mother's touch and had been looking forward to being properly alone. Surely they wouldn't really have to wait three whole days?

He swung his legs over the side of the bed and stood, and everything wobbled for just a moment. As he bent over the bed and clung on for support, Vasily was forced to concede that perhaps the maester knew his job after all.

Mother was at his side in an instant, one arm around Vasily's waist as he helped him sit on the side of the bed. "Are you sure he doesn't need to stay longer?" he asked, his brow creased with worry, and Vasily loved him a little more for his obvious concern.

"As I said, he's fit to go home as long as you watch him and he doesn't exert himself," Maester Owens repeated.

Vasily threw him a grateful smile. As nice as the infirmary was, he suspected he'd go mad being cooped up in it for too long. He stood again, more carefully this time, and to his relief there was no dizziness. He glanced down at his nightshirt and screwed up his face. "Am I walking to the cottage wearing this, then?" Another thought struck him. "Oh, bollocks."

"What is it?" Mother asked, the furrow in his brow deepening as he hovered. "Are you hurt? Do you need to be sick? You're very pale."

Vasily groaned. "No, nothing like that. But I left my good boots down at the harbour." He sat back down. "I don't suppose someone could run and collect them for me?"

Mother shook his head. "They'll be long gone. Mine too, probably."

With a look of disbelief, Vasily said, "What, you think somebody would just...take them?"

Mother shrugged, and a rueful smile tugged at his lips. "Nice pair of boots, sitting all alone on a wall? They're just begging to be pinched, aren't they? They were probably gone before you were out of the water."

"That's terrible!"

"That's life when you're not—"

Vasily saw the exact moment Mother bit back the work *royalty* with a sideways glance at the maester.

"Anyway, I'm sure I can rustle you up another pair. I'll fetch your clothes. You wait here." Mother ducked his head and stole a quick kiss before he disappeared out the door. It was barely a press of lips, but it still made Vasily's stomach flutter pleasantly.

While Mother was gone, Vasily made use of the privy, and when he came out, there was a shallow bathtub filled with steaming water. It was exactly what he hadn't known he needed. As Vasily smoothed a cloth covered in soap suds over his limbs and rinsed his hair, the maester kept a weather eye on him from a seat next to the tub. It turned out to be a good thing, because when he stood to get out, things got decidedly fuzzy for a second. But the maester was right there, holding his elbow and keeping him steady.

When Vasily sat on the edge of the bed to dry himself, he half expected the maester to say he wasn't fit to leave, but instead he just raised an eyebrow at him and said, "Perhaps *four* days."

Vasily gave a grateful nod, his shoulders slumping. He eyed the bed longingly, and his body reminded him that it had had quite the day and would like to lie down now, please. The plump feather pillow looked too good to resist, and Vasily didn't even try. He pulled the quilt back, slid underneath, and spent several minutes appreciating the soft texture of the bed linen as it brushed against his bare skin. It was a far cry from the rough sheets in his cottage.

He was just drifting off when the door opened, and a moment later the side of the bed dipped with the weight of someone sitting. He opened his eyes to find Mother looking down at him, an amused smile on his face. "Seems I was wrong, lad."

Vasily sat up and rubbed a hand over his eyes. "What?"

Mother bent down and picked something up off the floor and held it aloft. There, dangling from his fingertips by their knotted laces, were Vasily's boots. "Apparently, people aren't quite big enough bastards to rob a drowning man after all. Found these on your doorstep, along with mine." Mother wrinkled his nose. "Mind, they do both smell of horseshit, so mayhap nobody wanted them."

Vasily wasn't sure why he found the idea of his boots being too ripe to even steal funny—perhaps it was just because he was so tired. Regardless, he threw back his head and laughed, unable to help himself. Mother joined him, wrapping an arm around his bare shoulders and holding him close. And if somewhere along the way Vasily's hysterical laughter turned to tears, Mother was nice enough not to mention it.

Instead he held Vasily through it, running a soothing hand up and down his spine, and when his sobs had turned to hiccupping wet noises, Mother quietly stood and dipped the washcloth in the still-warm bath water, then wiped Vasily's face in sure, gentle strokes before drying it on the edge of a towel. "Better?"

Vasily nodded. He felt lighter, like he'd shed the turmoil of the day, and the tightness in his chest that had been there since he'd woken up had eased. He reached out and took Mother's hand, turning it over in his own before pressing a kiss to the palm. "Thank you."

Mother's eyes were full of warmth as he lifted their joined hands and kissed Vasily's knuckles. "Anything for you, love." He extracted his hand and pulled back the blankets. "We should get you dressed and home and leave Maester Owens in peace."

Vasily looked around, intending to thank the maester for his time, but the room was empty. "Where did he go?" He hadn't heard him leave.

Mother handed him his smallclothes. "I think he slipped out before, to give us some privacy."

"Oh," Vasily said faintly. "That was good of him."

He thought once more about what his father would say if he knew that Vasily had not only sobbed like a child but done it in front of the staff. It was lucky, he decided, that his father would never set foot in Lilleforth.

⁓

Mother took Vasily back to his cottage, an arm around his waist the entire time. Vasily was far more tired from the short walk than he felt he should be, but the sight of Mother's cottage with its big comfy bed and familiar faded quilt made the effort worth it.

Mother caught him yawning and wasted no time settling Vasily on the bed, and he rolled onto his front so he could bury his face in the bedding that smelled of Mother. Once the lamps had been lit and the fire stoked to a cheerful blaze, Mother lay down on the bed with him and ran his hands up and down Vasily's back in long, sweeping motions and soft touches that had his eyelids fluttering closed. Vasily wasn't sure how long he dozed for, but when he woke the cottage was filled with the aroma of beef stew. He ate greedily, and Mother gave him an approving nod when he asked for seconds.

After dinner, Mother ran his fingers through Vasily's hair and tutted at the state of it. He settled him next to the fireplace on a low stool, then sat behind him and carefully brushed all the knots and tangles out of his hair until the strands ran through his fingers like a waterfall, gleaming in the firelight. The tug of the hairbrush was soothing and hypnotic, and if Vasily had been a cat, he would have been purring. He settled for a low, throaty moan.

"You can't make noises like that, Vasily," Mother murmured, gathering his hair to one side and draping it over his shoulder. "Not if you expect me to follow the maester's orders."

Vasily tilted his head back and when he saw the heat in Mother's gaze, he preened inwardly.

Mother *wanted* him.

And Mother wasn't the only one who wanted. The food and sleep had gone a long way towards making Vasily feel more like himself, and Mother's hands running through his hair and over his skin had awakened a need in him for a more intimate touch.

He moved off the stool and straddled Mother's lap, and the way Mother's hands automatically settled at his hips and then traced up his sides was gratifying and arousing all at once. Vasily settled his forehead against Mother's. "Take me to bed, Bryn?" he said quietly. "I need to feel you."

Mother stilled. "I don't want to chance hurting you, Vasily. My heart couldn't take it."

Vasily pressed a soft kiss to his lips, and then another. "I don't want you to hurt me either. But I need to feel"—he didn't know how else to explain it, so he settled for—"*alive*. I want to touch your bare skin, feel it against mine. Please?"

Mother's hands tightened on his sides, just for a moment, before he breathed out a soft, *"Yes."* He leaned forward and began pressing kisses up the side of Vasily's throat, the rasp of his stubble and the tickle of warm breath making Vasily shiver with anticipation. He tipped his head to the side to allow better access, and when Mother slid his hands up Vasily's back and across his shoulders, setting his skin alight with his touch, Vasily rasped out, "Bed?"

Mother stood, pulled him to his feet, and led him to the bed. "You are the devil's own temptation, Vasily Petrov," he said, his eyes dark with arousal.

Vasily stripped out of his shirt and trousers and crawled under the quilt, and Mother followed him. He settled himself on top of Vasily, balancing on his elbows, and kissed him breathless. The heat of his mouth, the brush of bare skin, and the solid weight of Mother's body as he rocked his hips soon had Vasily's cock hard. He ran his hands over Mother's arse, kneading the flesh there, and Mother grunted and ground down, his hard shaft sliding against Vasily's and making his body sing with need. He whimpered and Mother stopped kissing him immediately, his eyes snapping open and his body stilling. "Love?"

Vasily let out a breathless laugh. "I'm fine. It just feels so good."

Mother gave a relieved smile, and a second later his expression turned filthy and mischievous all at once. "Just to be safe, you should let me do all the work." And with that he slid down the bed and took Vasily's cock in his mouth.

Vasily jolted, arching up into the unexpected heat and delicious friction as Mother slid his mouth up and down his shaft, sucking and licking and swirling his tongue in ways that had Vasily's cock aching. He whined high in his throat and clutched at Mother's hair, and Mother chuckled around his length.

The vibrations took Vasily's breath away as he was consumed by the soft, wet heat of Mother's mouth and the rasp of his tongue against the sensitive head of Vasily's cock. Tension coiled in his gut, tighter and tighter, and heat crackled down his spine and set his entire body alight. He couldn't help himself, using Mother's hair to hold him in place as he thrust desperately into his mouth. Mother's response was to hollow his cheeks and suck harder, and when he cupped Vasily's balls and gave a light tug, the sharp sting of it was all it took.

His cock pulsed without warning, and he spilled into Mother's mouth.

Pleasure rolled over him, intense and unstoppable, until he was shaking with it, and his world was reduced to the white heat of his release.

Mother eased him through it, and when Vasily was done, cock soft and spent, he moved up the bed and lay next to Vasily, cradling him against his chest and kissing his temple. Vasily melted into his hold, and reached out and trailed his hand across Mother's stomach, searching. Mother's erection slapped against his belly, the tip slippery and damp, and Vasily rubbed his hand across the tip before moving it up and down the shaft, spreading the moisture.

"That's it," Mother said breathlessly. "Won't take much."

Vasily hummed, enjoying the caress of velvet skin against his palm, and gave a series of slow, lazy strokes that had Mother letting out a low groan and arching up into his touch. The corded muscles of his throat stood out in stark relief where his head was thrown back, eyes closed and lips parted.

Mother was breathtaking when he was desperate.

Teasing the tip of his thumb over the glistening head, Vasily tightened his grip and gave a single stroke, and that was all it took. Mother tensed against him, making the most glorious noises as he painted white stripes on his belly. Vasily held his softening cock while Mother panted and shuddered through his orgasm, and when he finally let go, Mother collapsed against the mattress.

Vasily wiped the traces of Mother's release on a corner of the bedding, then rolled over onto his back beside him and let out a contented sigh, taking a moment to enjoy the fact that he could take Mother apart so easily.

Their lovemaking had settled something in him, a deep,

instinctive need to celebrate life in the oldest of ways that he hadn't been able to find words for. It had been exactly what he'd needed.

He reached out and tangled his fingers in Mother's, squeezing his hand and giving him a wordless look of thanks. When Mother's eyelids drifted closed a minute later, he was still wearing a lazy smile, and it wasn't long before his breathing settled into a slow, regular pattern.

It occurred to Vasily, just before the post-sex haze of sleep pulled him under, that really, it was Mother that he'd needed all along.

Chapter Seventeen

Mother couldn't help but feel there was a kind of rightness to having Vasily living in his house.

Vasily didn't *actually* live with him, of course. He just...hadn't left after he'd first stayed the night. At first it was because Mother had wanted to be certain Vasily really was recovered from his head injury—he'd seen more than one case where a hoof to the head had turned nasty days or even weeks later, and Vasily *had* taken a fair knock.

But Vasily had turned out to be fine, so there was no reason for him still to be staying at Mother's ten days later. Yet more and more of Vasily's possessions were making their way into his cottage—Mother pretended not to notice—and there was no mention of when Vasily might be leaving.

Possibly it was because they were both perfectly happy with the arrangement and neither of them wanted to call a stop to it. Mother was certainly in no hurry, not when his days and nights were now filled with Vasily's smile, his laughter, and his eager kisses.

One of Mother's favourite things about living with Vasily

was waking up tangled in Vasily's embrace or with his face resting against Vasily's firmly muscled chest.

Another new favourite pastime was waking Vasily up by sucking his brains out through his cock. A kiss probably would have sufficed, but Mother found that when it came to Vasily, he couldn't get enough of bedding him, touching him, pleasing him. It was almost as if Mother was trying to make up for all of the sex he'd missed in his twenties—except he didn't feel he *had* missed out, because he hadn't *wanted* to bed anyone before now.

He only wanted Vasily. He was intoxicating, sweeter than wine and far more addictive, and Mother had no intention of giving him up.

He stood watching Vasily, who was currently helping him haul sacks of feed off a cart and stacking them inside the stables. He was shirtless, his every movement making his muscles bunch and flex temptingly. Mother was fairly certain the show was for his benefit, and it was certainly a pretty display.

He wondered again how it was that only *this* man appealed to him. He'd seen plenty of strapping lads over the years, and none of them had affected him like Vasily did.

He watched for a minute more before deciding that he didn't really care about the why. The important thing was that he and Vasily fit together as perfectly as a dovetail joint, two pieces slipping easily into place, becoming one.

He smiled to himself and went back to work, carrying sacks and stacking them with the ease of twenty-odd years' experience, and soon enough the cart was empty. All around them, Mother's stable boys and grooms were working hard, diligently sweeping and shovelling and cleaning, just like he'd taught them. It filled him with a sense of pride, and as he walked the length of the stables, he made sure to deliver words of encouragement.

When he got to Ollie, who was tending to Crown Prince Davin's mount and cooing sweet nothings at the horse, he remembered his earlier decision. "Ollie, lad, got a minute?"

Ollie's head snapped up, his eyes wide. "Of course, Mister Jones, only can I just finish up here? I'm nearly done."

Mother nodded approvingly. Ollie's determination to finish what he'd started was confirmation of the rightness of his choice. Soon enough the horse had been turned out to pasture, and Ollie came and stood in front of him, hands clasped behind his back, spine ramrod straight. He bit his bottom lip before blurting out, "Am I in trouble?"

Mother reached out and patted his shoulder reassuringly. "Not at all, lad. The opposite. Come walk with me?"

Ollie let out a long breath and his shoulders slumped in relief. Leading him into the side room where they polished the tack, Mother gestured for him to sit down at the wooden table.

Mother took the other chair, clasping his hands in front of him. "Do you like working with the horses, lad?"

Ollie nodded so vigorously that a shower of straw fell from his hair. "Yessir."

Mother grinned at his enthusiasm. He'd thought about teasing the boy before delivering his news but found he couldn't do it. "How would you feel about being apprenticed as a groom?"

A squeak escaped as Ollie's mouth dropped open. Mother grinned and waited, and eventually Ollie managed to gather himself enough to say, "That'd be bloody brilliant!"

"That's a yes, then? It's four years, mind."

"I know, I mean, yes, I mean, please!" Ollie's leg jiggled with excitement, and his face split into a wide smile. "Do you really mean it? You really want me?"

"Can't think of anyone better," Mother said, standing. "We'll get it sorted with the steward tomorrow, and you can start your proper training next week."

"Thank you," Ollie said, his voice hoarse. He stood quivering with excitement and dancing from one foot to the other. "Can I tell my mum and dad?"

"Course you can, lad." Mother had already discussed his plans with King Leopold, and they'd agreed Ollie was a good choice, so there was no reason for him not to share his news. "In fact, once you're done here, you can go home and tell them."

Ollie was on his feet in a second. "Thank you! I wanted, I mean, I'd hoped—" He stopped mid-sentence and launched himself at Mother, throwing his arms around him and whispering another hoarse, "Thank you!" as he squeezed him tight.

Mother laughed and squeezed the boy back once before making a shooing motion. "Off you go. I'll see you bright and early tomorrow."

Ollie beamed at him before practically bouncing out the door with excitement. By the time Mother stepped out of the room, he was long gone.

Mother looked around, but Vasily was nowhere to be seen, so he walked around to the stables where Blackbird and Shadow were kept. Even though the horses had been put out to pasture, Vasily was there sitting on a low stool, his back against a stall door, elbows resting on his spread knees. He looked relaxed and happy, his head tipped back and eyes closed, but they snapped open when Mother approached, and he grinned. "I just saw Ollie go racing past like his arse was on fire. What did you do?"

Mother shrugged. "Told him I'd apprentice him."

Vasily's face split into a grin that was, if possible, wider than Ollie's had been. "You do know that was his dream?"

"I had an inkling," Mother said with a smile, "and he's a good choice, so why not give him what he wants?"

Vasily stood and stretched, giving Mother a glimpse of the skin of his belly, and Mother found himself recalling last night, when he'd pinned Vasily to the bed and pressed soft kisses all over his hips and stomach before stroking them both off, fast and urgent, and collapsing in a sweaty, satisfied heap.

Heat surged through him at the memory, and he wondered

if he could get away with dragging Vasily back to their cottage and doing it all again.

He blinked.

Their cottage.

Suddenly, he wanted that desperately.

"Mother?" Vasily laid a hand on his cheek. "Are you all right?"

Mother placed a hand over Vasily's. "Aye, I just...would you..." He hesitated. They hadn't talked about the future. They hadn't even talked about Vasily's royal status, deliberately choosing to ignore it for now. Yet here Mother was, seized with the desire to ask Vasily to live with him like a proper couple. Surely, the very idea was madness.

But then again, wasn't courting a prince its own kind of madness?

Mother leaned into Vasily's touch and caught his gaze, and the concern and affection he saw there decided him. Every step of the way, Vasily had been the one to take the lead.

Perhaps this time, Mother could be the bold one.

He settled one hand on Vasily's shoulder, just to keep himself steady. "I was wondering if you would...stay. With me."

Vasily's brow creased in confusion. "Stay?"

"At my house. With me. All the time. Properly." Mother's heart thundered against his ribs, and he forgot how to breathe as he waited.

Vasily bit his lip. "You don't want me to go back to my own cottage?"

Mother shook his head mutely.

Vasily stared for a second, then grinned widely. "I don't want to go back either," he said. "I want to stay with you."

It took a moment for the words to sink in, but when they did, Mother took Vasily's face in his hands and kissed him, exhilaration fluttering in his chest like a flock of birds desperate to fly free. He pulled back and let out a breathless laugh, unable to hold it in.

Vasily let out a pleased sound and ran one hand down Mother's spine, making him shiver. "Shall I bring the rest of my things over tonight?"

Mother nodded, then lifted his head and asked, "What things, lad?"

"Well, there's my clothes and spare boots—no, wait, they're already there. But I have a towel and a washcloth, except—" Vasily stopped mid-sentence, and Mother waited for him to catch up. "Mother," he asked, eyes wide, "have I already moved in?"

Mother grinned so hard his cheeks ached. "As good as, love."

It was Vasily's turn to laugh, the sound echoing through the stables, and Mother joined him, feeling lighter than he ever had. He didn't know how this was going to work with Vasily still being an heir to the Koroslovan throne, and he wasn't sure how he'd cope when the time came for him to leave, but he shoved those thoughts to the back of his mind.

Vasily was his, for now at least, and if his being a prince meant that this turned out to be temporary, then Mother was determined to make the most of it while he could.

They'd worry about the rest of it later.

∼

Mother spent several hours that afternoon up at the castle with the steward, sorting out Ollie's apprenticeship and arranging to hire a new stable boy to replace him. Perhaps it was because he was impatient to get back to Vasily and get him moved in properly, but everything seemed to take twice as long it should. Finally, though, the arrangements were made, and Mother was able to make his escape.

The sun was low in the sky by the time he got back, and

when he checked the main stables, his grooms were just finishing up for the day, with all the horses fed and in their stalls. He checked their work and dismissed them, leaving him alone with the fragrance of hay and horse sweat. He made his way to the royal stalls, and when he stuck his head around the door, Vasily had his back to him. He was stroking Blackbird's nose and talking softly to her, completely oblivious to Mother's presence. His shirt was untucked with his sleeves rolled up to his elbows, and shadows danced across his body, making him appear longer and leaner than he was. His hair was loose, tumbling down over his shoulders.

He was beautiful.

"Are you going to stand there all day staring at my arse?" Vasily said, turning his head and flashing Mother a grin.

Perhaps it was the way the loose strands of Vasily's hair danced around his face, or perhaps it was the way he licked his bottom lip, teasing, but Mother was seized by an urge to claim him. Without stopping to think, he marched forward and grabbed Vasily around the waist, hoisting him over his shoulder where he dangled like a sack of feed.

Vasily's breath caught and he fell silent, and Mother stopped dead, suddenly afraid he'd crossed some line he wasn't aware of. "Vas?" he said quietly, setting him gently down. He wasn't sure what he was expecting, but it wasn't for Vasily's cheeks to be flushed or his eyes to be glittering with lust. "You just lifted me like I weighed nothing," Vasily rasped. "I liked it."

Oh.

Mother raised an eyebrow and grinned, swinging Vasily over his shoulder again and giving his arse a playful slap as he spun on his heel towards the door. "Is that so? Shall I carry you back to—"

He stopped in his tracks when an unfamiliar man swept through the doorway, a fur-trimmed cloak swirling behind him. He was tall and broad with a straight nose, square features, and long hair that was greying at the temples. His clothing was well cut if travel worn, and his stance was that of a man who wielded power. He was obviously nobility of some sort, and the question of his identity was answered when, from somewhere down by Mother's right arse cheek, Vasily squeaked out, "*Father?*"

Mother stared wide-eyed, and seconds later the man was joined by a slim dark-haired woman who was also wearing a fur-trimmed cloak and also holding herself impeccably upright, despite the dust of travel clinging to the hem of her dress.

"Oh gods," Vasily whispered.

Mother's gut curdled. Standing in front of him was King Alexei of Koroslova—reportedly the sternest figure in six kingdoms—and there Mother was with the man's son slung over his shoulder like some tipsy tavern wench.

His face burned hot, and he hurried to set Vasily on his feet as he scrambled to think of an explanation for what the king and queen had just seen.

But Alexei seemed not to have noticed Mother at all. All his focus was on Vasily. He looked him up and down for a moment, then stepped forward and dragged him into a crushing hug. "My Vasily," he choked out. "You're *alive*."

There was a flurry of movement and then the woman— Queen Irina— threw her arms around Vasily as well, scolding him as she did so. "You were supposed to be safe here! Not throw yourself into the sea!" she tutted. "You frightened us!"

Vasily was wide-eyed and pale, but despite that he was beaming. "What are you doing here?" he asked as he finally extracted himself from his mother's arms.

"What do you *mean*, what are we doing here?" his father said. "You were injured, and you thought we wouldn't come and check on you? You are our *son.*"

"Yes, but it was just an accident," Vasily said. "I'm fine, I swear."

The king swept Vasily up in an enormous bear hug,

swinging him around and lifting him off the ground with the force of it before smiling broadly and letting him go. "You seem fit and well. At least well enough for some horseplay," he said with a nod at Vasily and Mother. "It is good to see boys being boys."

It was in that moment that Mother realised King Alexei had *no* idea his son liked men. He obviously assumed they'd been indulging in nothing more than a bit of innocent foolishness, the sort of thing young boys were prone to—never mind that it had been a long time since anyone had mistaken Mother for a boy.

"Horseplay, yes," Vasily echoed. His pale face regained some colour as he obviously came to the same conclusion about his father's obliviousness.

"I wrestled when I was younger," King Alexei said, patting Vasily on the back. "Makes the blood race."

Vasily's mother looked Mother up and down, assessing. "And who is your...friend, Vasily?"

"Mother."

"Yes?" the queen said, a touch impatiently.

"No, Mother. He's Mother. I mean, um. Mother, this is Mother Jones." Vasily touched Mother's sleeve before dropping his hand to his side.

A silence fell.

"Your name is...Mother?" the queen asked, her brow creased.

Both the king and queen turned towards him as one, and Mother fought the urge to hide in one of the stalls under the intensity of their stare. Instead, falling back on years of experience, he cleared his throat, laced his fingers behind his back, and with a small bow, declared, "Mother Jones at your service, Your Majesties."

"He saved my life," Vasily said eagerly. "He's the one who fished me out of the harbour." He rested his hand on Mother's shoulder, and his touch lingered slightly longer than it should have before he removed it.

King Alexei's eyes widened. "You saved our son?"

"Aye, sire. Saw him fall, and I couldn't lose my best groom," Mother said, hoping to lighten the moment.

King Alexei's mouth curved up into a broad smile that held echoes of Vasily in it, and in two strides he was at Mother's side, slapping him on the back so hard Mother wondered that the teeth didn't come flying out of his mouth. "Excellent man!" he exclaimed.

"Thank you, sire," Mother wheezed.

"We shall have King Leopold host a dinner for you," Alexei declared, "in thanks."

"Oh, bugger off," Mother said, before slapping a hand over his mouth, horrified. Had he *actually* just cursed in front of the king and queen of Koroslova? He swallowed. "I meant to say, if that's what Your Majesty wishes, sire."

King Alexei gave an amused huff. "Excellent. We will arrange it. Now, who will tend to our horses after their trip?"

Mother almost heaved a sigh of relief. That, he could do. "I will, sire." He stepped towards the courtyard and Vasily went to follow him. The king put a hand on his son's arm. "Where are you going, Vasily?"

"To tend the horses, Father. It's my job."

His father shook his head. "Nonsense. We did not ride all this way for you to run off with the horses. Come, we will go up to the castle and you can tell us about your time here over dinner."

It didn't sound like a request, and Vasily's shoulders slumped.

"It's fine, lad," Mother said quietly. "I'll get it sorted." He forced a smile and tried to ignore the hollow ache inside of him that whispered that this was it, this was where Vasily realised that Mother wasn't right for a prince.

His hands twitched at his side with the need to reach out and take Vasily's hand to reassure them both, but of course it was impossible. He clenched them into fists instead, lest he reach out and give away their secret.

King Alexei threw an arm around Vasily's shoulder and led him out of the stables, the queen on his other side, and Mother was left alone.

∼

Looking around the empty stable yard, Mother wondered if he was meant to walk up to the castle to fetch the horses and how many were in the royal contingent, but before he had a chance to go anywhere, there was the familiar clatter of hooves and he looked to see Janus riding slowly towards him leading a horse on each side. When he reached the yard, he handed Mother the reins to his extra mounts before sliding off the saddle with a groan.

He had bags under his eyes, and he winced as he reached around and rubbed the small of his back. "I'm getting too old for this," he grumbled. "Ten days in the saddle, and I'm ready to sleep for a week."

Mother looked past him at the empty road. "Where are the rest of them? Still at the castle?"

Janus set a hand on the saddle and leaned against it, giving Mother a wry smile. "It's just the king and queen. They left the horses and came straight to the stables. They haven't even properly greeted Leo and Felix yet. When I told them what had happened to Vasily, they couldn't leave Koroslova to get here fast enough. Didn't bother with a retinue and told me that if I was good enough to guard the King of Lilleforth, I was good enough for them." He stretched and winced. "I had one night's sleep in a decent bed before we started back at first light the next day."

Mother didn't know why he was surprised. His own parents

would have done the same. It was just that somehow, in his mind, he'd painted Vasily's parents to be as cold as the country they came from.

Janus must have read his expression. "They love their son, even if his father doesn't quite understand him."

Mother cleared his throat and said quietly, "Do you think they know about..."

Janus made a seesawing motion with one hand. "It wouldn't even cross King Alexei's mind, but Queen Irina? I wouldn't be surprised. She was the one who arranged his position here, after all."

"Aye, she seems like she doesn't miss a trick, that one," Mother said, his mouth pressed into a thin line.

"Oh?" Janus tilted his head. "Did she see something?"

Mother looked skyward while he debated whether to say anything, but Janus was his friend, after all. "When they walked in, I had Vasily slung over my shoulder, and I was slapping his arse." His cheeks burned at the memory.

Janus threw his head back and laughed like the unsympathetic bastard he was.

"It's not funny," Mother grumbled.

Janus clapped a hand on his shoulder. "Sorry, Mother, but it really is. How did you explain it?"

He blew out a long breath. "Didn't need to. King Alexei thought we were just playing silly buggers. A bit of innocent horseplay."

Janus grinned. "Is the king blind?"

Mother gave a wry smile in return because it was *almost* funny. "I think maybe he is when it suits him."

One of the horses he was holding huffed in his ear, a reminder that Mother had a job to do. "I'd best get on," he said.

Janus took his leave, and Mother turned and led the royal mounts up the path to the general stables. But as he fed and groomed the horses and settled them in their stalls, he thought of Vasily, who, instead of working alongside him, was currently up at the castle living the life of a prince. Mother desperately wanted to believe that somehow there might be a place for *him* in that life.

But try as he might, he couldn't see how he'd fit.

Chapter Eighteen

Vasily hadn't realised how much he'd missed his parents until he saw them. Of course, he would have preferred to see them when he *wasn't* draped over Mother's shoulder, the slap to his arse still echoing around the stables, but luckily his father had interpreted what they were doing as some kind of harmless camaraderie, and Vasily wasn't about to correct him.

And now, with both of them walking beside him, he couldn't deny the warmth he felt inside knowing that he was loved enough for them both to abandon their kingdom and ride all the way here. At the same time, he felt a pang of guilt because it hadn't even occurred to him that they might be worried. Once Leopold had told him that Janus was riding to deliver the news that he'd had a fall but was safe and well, he'd assumed that would be the end of it.

But here they were, leading him up to the castle like they thought he lived there, and he wondered how he was going to break it to them that he was actually staying in a one-room cottage with an outside privy.

"—luncheon, don't you agree, Vasily?"

"What?" He blinked, and his mother sighed.

"I was just saying to Alexei, I know he wants to thank Mister Jones, but a formal banquet might be too much for the poor man, so why not have a light luncheon? Just us and the king and prince consort and the crown prince—and you, of course. I get the feeling your Mister Jones won't want anything more than that."

Alexei gave his wife a soft smile. "Whatever you think is best, my love." Vasily wasn't surprised—he could count on the fingers of one hand the number of times his father had said no to his queen.

"A luncheon sounds perfect," he said. "Mother's not much for ceremony or crowds."

"We will arrange it with King Leopold." His mother took Vasily's hand and slowed her steps so that they fell in behind the king, and when there was enough distance, she lowered her voice and asked, "So, this Mister Jones, is he your friend?"

Vasily nodded.

The queen clasped his hand more tightly in both of hers. "And is he what people might call a *special* friend?"

Vasily hesitated, but he never had been able to keep a secret from his mother—even one as big as this. His throat bobbed as he swallowed hard before whispering, "Yes."

He held his breath, waiting for her response, and he almost collapsed with relief when she nodded to herself as if confirming something, then said, "I think I like your new friend. He seems like a good man."

"He is," Vasily said. "The very best."

And he really was. Vasily had never known anybody like Mother, with his crooked smile and accidental innuendos and soft heart and strong hands. Not to mention his kissable lips and very pretty cock.

"Vasily?" his mother said quietly, and he snapped out of his thoughts to find that they'd reached the courtyard and were standing in front of the main entrance to the castle.

After all the months coming in through the side gate near the laundry, it felt strange to be using the wide double doors, but Vasily squared his shoulders and, with a nod at the guards, led his parents inside.

Leo and Felix were waiting with welcoming smiles, and Leo stepped forward and greeted Vasily's parents with a half bow. "King Alexei, Queen Irina, welcome to Lilleforth. You are most welcome here." He was the picture of royal composure, and there was no sign of the man who only yesterday Vasily had seen squabbling with Felix over the last cream cake, a tussle which had ended up with him licking cream off his husband's fingers.

Queen Irina gave a curtsy and King Alexei returned the bow, saying, "We are most thankful for your hospitality."

"Of course," Leopold said and beamed like the gracious host he was.

Felix stood silently beside Leopold, his hands clasped behind his back like the perfect prince consort, and as pleasantries were exchanged and dinner plans made, it occurred to Vasily that it was rather like watching an intricate dance—except all the steps were taught from birth, and heaven help anyone who joined in late. He'd personally always found the ins and outs of protocol stifling, and he thought briefly of Mother and his statement that he wouldn't be caught getting involved with royalty. He wondered if Mother would ever be willing to take part in something like this.

And more to the point, could Vasily ask it of him?

Before dinner Vasily took the time to wash his face, tidy his hair, and smooth out the front of his shirt, and when he sat down at the table, he almost looked respectable.

It was agreed that a luncheon in Mother's honour the next day was fitting, and Vasily volunteered to go and deliver the news after dinner.

Although Vasily could tell his father wasn't exactly comfortable dining with a king who had a husband, he had to admire the way he conducted himself. He kept the conversation light and genial, discussing such scintillating topics as the crops, the weather, the state of the roads on their trip, and wasn't the meal tasty? There was a moment when Felix mentioned "my husband" and Alexei opened his mouth to say something, but his wife silenced him with a hard stare, and overall the evening went smoothly enough.

And yet, as Vasily ate his venison and drank his wine, he found himself thinking longingly of the mutton stew that Mother had planned to make.

When the meal was over, his parents retired early, tired from their journey. Vasily loved them, but he still heaved a sigh of relief. He was exhausted after his long workday, and being on his best behaviour all evening had been more taxing than he remembered. He was reminded once again why he'd spent most of his time hanging around the stables as a boy.

Once the table had been cleared, Vasily drummed his fingertips on the tabletop, wondering how to take his leave without sounding rude.

Felix saved him the trouble by standing and stretching. "Apologies, Vasily, but we're deserting you and going to bed."

"Are we?" Leopold asked.

Felix extended a hand to his husband. "King Alexei doubtless assumes we're getting up to all sorts of debauched behaviour tonight," he said. "It would be a shame to disappoint him."

"Oh! Well, if there's debauchery, I'm in," Leo said, a gleam in his eye. "Goodnight, Vasily. Say hello to Mother for me."

And then they were gone, laughter floating along in their wake, and Vasily didn't waste any time darting out the door. He was looking forward to getting back to his—no, *their*—cottage, spooning up behind Mother, and getting comfortable in his own skin again.

He hurried down the path, not slowing until he saw the lamplight gleaming through the small window as the cottage came into view. He opened the door quietly.

Mother spun around in his chair and his eyes lit up. "You came back! I thought you'd be staying at the castle."

"Why would I stay there when I live here?" Vasily said. He was rewarded with a bright smile, and all the tension of the evening fell away when Mother stood and stepped forward, cradled the back of his head, and kissed him. The taste of him was as welcome and refreshing as cool water on a summer's day, and Vasily closed his eyes and savoured the closeness as they kissed long and slow.

Eventually they parted, and Mother asked, "How was dinner?"

"It was good to see my family," Vasily said. "But I'd forgotten how much work protocol was."

"Sooner you than me," Mother said.

"About that. You're expected for luncheon at the castle tomorrow."

Vasily half expected Mother to refuse, but he just gave a resigned smile. "I suppose I'll have to polish my boots and dress my best, then."

"You don't mind?"

Mother settled his hands on Vasily's hips and leaned their

foreheads together. "Course I don't mind. It's lunch, not a hanging. And I can mind my manners easily enough."

Vasily bit back a smile. "You mean when you're not telling the king to bugger off?"

"He caught me off guard!" Mother huffed.

Vasily opened his mouth to say something, but it turned into a yawn.

"Come to bed, love," Mother said.

"I don't know if I can sleep," Vasily admitted. He was tired, but his mind was whirling with unanswered questions. What, exactly, were his parents doing here? How long were they staying? What would happen if his father realised he and Mother were more than friends? What if seeing Vasily in his role as prince meant Mother no longer wanted him?

"Shhh," Mother murmured against the side of his throat, running a broad palm up and down his side in a soothing motion as if he could sense his unease. Perhaps he could. "I know just the way to help you relax."

He tugged Vasily's shirt over his head and Vasily unlaced his trousers, and once they were both undressed, they climbed into bed. Mother guided him onto his back and settled himself on top of Vasily, and the heat and weight of him as he rolled his hips in a gentle rhythm was perfect for distracting Vasily from his thoughts. Mother nipped and kissed at the side of his throat while he wrapped a hand around both of their cocks and worked them slow and easy to their climax, and it wasn't long before Vasily spilled with a sigh, Mother following close behind.

He lay there afterwards, mind pleasantly fuzzy while Mother wiped them down, and as Mother plastered himself along the length of his spine, Vasily couldn't help but feel that perhaps everything would work out all right after all.

Vasily squirmed as he tugged at the collar of his deep grey doublet and wondered once again if he could get away with a clean shirt and trousers. He sighed, knowing the answer. Today he was Prince Vasily, fifth in line for the throne of Koroslova, and his parents would expect him to dress accordingly.

He brushed at the front of his fitted midnight blue trousers, which seemed far too constricting to be healthy. He knew it was just his imagination—if anything he was leaner now than when he'd arrived—but he still felt like a heap of straw stuffed into a sack that was one size too small.

He sighed again.

It was only for one day.

Mother had assured Vasily that once he'd sorted the stables out and assigned the grooms their tasks, he'd be back to wash and change. Part of Vasily felt that he should be helping in the stables as well instead of standing here fiddling with the collar of his best doublet, but Mother had assured him it was fine.

He ran a hand through his hair and a smile crept onto his face. Mother had brushed the tangles out for him this morning with long, slow strokes that had felt like a caress, and now it fell in silken strands between his fingers. He was tempted to leave it loose, but he could imagine the disapproving looks of his father, so he took the time to braid it. His parents would be expecting him to look his best, and he had to admit that seeing them again almost made dressing up worth it.

Almost.

Hair done, he picked up the looking glass from the table and regarded his handiwork. With his hair tied back and his face shaved bare of the rough stubble he'd been sporting, there was no denying that he looked every inch a prince. He put the mirror down and ignored the voice that whispered, *because you are.*

The door opened. "Oh, just look at you, love."

Vasily turned to find Mother gazing at him, and some of his discomfort eased in the face of Mother's undisguised admiration. He gave a small formal bow, a smile playing around his lips. "Prince Vasily Anatoly Alexei Pasha Petrov, at your service."

Mother grinned. "We can get to the servicing later. First, I have to get ready for this bloody lunch."

Vasily laughed, his nerves easing, and it didn't take Mother long to wash, brush his own wayward locks with more care than normal, and dress in a well-fitted shirt and trousers that made him look rather dashing.

The day was cool but the skies were clear, and Vasily soaked up the tentative rays of sunshine as he walked up to the castle with Mother by his side. He kept his hands clasped behind his back, aware that otherwise he was just as likely to reach out and hold Mother's hand. He could only imagine the chaos that would set loose if his father saw.

They ducked in the side gate at the castle, but instead of taking the turn to the left that led to the kitchens for lunch like they usually did, they veered to the right along the passageway that led to the formal dining room.

When they entered it was to find King Alexei, Prince Consort Felix, and Crown Prince Davin standing in a cluster next to a long, oval table that could easily have held a dozen guests. Vasily sensed Mother hesitating next to him, and he desperately wanted to reach out and touch him, offer some reassurance, but he couldn't. He wondered if being a prince of Koroslova would always mean being unable to reach for the one he loved.

He wondered, not for the first time, if it was worth it.

"Vasily!" His father turned, stepping forward and embracing him. Then he turned to Mother and extended a broad palm in a welcoming gesture. "And the man who saved him, Mister Jones the stablemaster!"

Mother stepped forward, giving a polite bow and murmuring, "Sire," before stepping back.

Just then King Leopold and Queen Irina entered the room, Leopold grinning wickedly and the queen letting out a tinkling laugh. She glided over to her husband, taking his elbow and bestowing a smile on him, and as always, Alexei's face melted into a hapless smile as he gazed into her eyes. Vasily had never been able to understand how his father's demeanour could instantly transform into something soft and sweet at the merest touch of his mother's hand. But now, glancing over at Mother, he thought he just might.

"Shall we sit?" Leopold suggested, and they assembled around the table—Vasily, Mother, and Davin along one side, and Felix, Alexei, and Irina along the other. Felix was seated to the right of Leopold, who, of course, sat at the head of the table.

It was strange watching Leopold act like royalty when Vasily was far more used to seeing him at the kitchen tables laughing over some joke he'd made, or watching him beg Cook for a slice of her hangover cake while he swore never to drink again and Felix mocked him.

Once they were seated, the food was brought in, and much like the night before, the conversation was careful and polite. Vasily kept an eye on Mother, who remained quiet, pushing his food around his plate and looking less like an honoured guest and more like a man for the gallows, despite what he'd said the night before. Not that Vasily could blame him—even on his best behaviour, his father's personality was overwhelming. He longed to lean over and kiss Mother's cheek and whisper reassurances in his ear or at least press their thighs together under the table, but he didn't dare.

Vasily himself was finding that, although familiar, the formality he was required to adopt over dinner didn't sit right anymore, rather like the clothing he wore, itching and chafing in ways he'd forgotten. When he thought of a future that consisted of endless occasions like this, his own appetite departed and he found himself shoving his own food around his plate.

They were four courses in, and Vasily was busy wondering how much longer until they could escape and dreaming about taking Mother back to the cottage and peeling him out of those well-fitting trousers when his father said, "Of course, Vasily, we must discuss your return to Koroslova."

"Sorry, what?" he said, his head whipping up from his plate.

His father regarded him, steely-eyed. "Your return. When we heard about your accident, it made me realise..." He paused and, unbelievably, swiped the back of one hand over his eyes. Glaring around the table, he dared anyone to say anything before continuing. "I miss you, as does your mother. I feel you should come home and take up your role as a prince of the realm."

Vasily stared, his heart thundering in his chest as he tried to make sense of what his father was saying. "But...a-a year," he stammered. "I-I had a year to travel and see the world. You agreed."

His father raised a stern eyebrow. "But you are *not* seeing the world. You are working like a commoner in the stables in Lilleforth."

"But—"

"There are far more fitting roles for a prince than a groom, and you will be safe in Koroslova," his father said firmly. "Perhaps we shall even arrange a marriage. A nice princess."

Blood roared in Vasily's ears, and he felt sick to his stomach. His first instinct was to look over at Mother, who had gone sheet white.

"I don't want a princess," he said, teeth gritted.

"Not right away, of course," his father continued, and Vasily couldn't decide if he was oblivious or just used to getting his own way. "We shall say in a month, when the weather is better for travelling. Are we agreed?"

Vasily stared at him, unable to believe what his father was saying. *A month?*

He looked again at Mother, who caught his gaze, his eyes wet, and it was then that Vasily felt it.

Mother pressed his thigh against Vasily's under the table, solid and comforting. That was Mother all over—looking after Vasily even in the midst of his own distress. Vasily tried to remember the last time someone had cared for him the way Mother did, and he couldn't.

He loved his family, but he loved Mother too. It was an impossible choice.

"Mother," he said softly—and gods, how unfair of him was it to even ask? "Mother, what should I do?"

Chapter Nineteen

Don't you bloody well cry.

Mother set his jaw and swallowed around the lump in his throat, determined not to let his emotions get the better of him. If he cried, King Alexei would have questions, and Mother wasn't about to cost Vasily his place in the Koroslovan royal family because he couldn't hold back a few bloody tears.

Even if his heart *was* being torn out of his chest.

But he couldn't stop himself from leaning into Vasily, their thighs pressed together under the table, and putting a hand on Vasily's leg in one last, illicit touch.

Vasily blinked rapidly and then, glancing down at where Mother's hand was resting on his thigh, seemed to steel himself. He straightened his spine, stuck his chest out, looked his father in the eye, and said, "No."

Mother's breath caught.

No?

Vasily couldn't be choosing him. Could he?

Then Vasily slipped a hand under the table, put it on top of

Mother's, and squeezed—and that, that told Mother all he needed to know.

King Alexei tilted his head, his brow creased as if he had trouble understanding. "But...you need to come home. Take your place."

Vasily jutted his chin out. "I said no. I want to stay here."

The king's eyebrows raised, and his face started to go an alarming shade of purple right before he slammed his fist on the table. "You do not say no to me! Why would you possibly want to stay here?"

"I like it here," Vasily said, his voice shaking. "I have...friends here."

"Friends?" Alexei roared, standing and towering over Vasily. "You are disobeying your king for *friends?*"

Mother had to wrap the hand not settled on Vasily's leg around the edge of the chair to stop from launching himself across the table and punching Alexei in the face, king or no, because *nobody* spoke to his Vasily like that.

"Alexei."

The queen's voice rang out like a whipcrack, and Alexei stiffened at the sound of it. Mother dared to glance her way, only to find Irina sitting calm and collected, one eyebrow raised, with her gaze fixed on her husband—who, it appeared, was sitting down.

"Better," Irina said. "There is no need for such *drama*, Alexei."

Despite himself, a choked laugh escaped Mother. Next to him, Vasily turned and gave him a small hopeful smile, and Mother got the feeling that perhaps he'd underestimated Queen Irina.

Leopold turned to the king and let out a loud sigh. "Honestly, Alexei, I feel for you. There's nothing worse than a wayward child who doesn't step up to their responsibilities. Especially a prince who won't pull their weight."

Mother stiffened and hoped like hell that Leopold wasn't going to insist Vasily leave, because that would mean Mother would be forced to punch *two* kings in a single day, and he wasn't sure he could cope with that.

But he would, if it came to it.

Alexei, sensing he had an ally, nodded. "They don't understand the meaning of responsibility."

"Quite," Leopold agreed. "They're quite feckless when left to their own devices. I've experienced it myself, in fact."

"Oh?" Alexei sat forward, interested now.

"Mother Jones," Leopold drawled casually, like there wasn't a power struggle going on around the dining table. "My own son, Davin, worked for you as a stable boy, correct?"

Mother's brow creased in confusion. What did Davin have to do with Vasily leaving? "You know he did, sire."

"What—" Felix started to say. Leopold held a hand up for silence.

Felix closed his mouth with a snap, and Leopold continued as if the interruption had never happened. "And what was he like as a worker, Mother?" He caught Mother's eye and something like mischief flashed across his face, there and gone again.

Mother was suddenly reminded that King Leopold was known for being an *excellent* diplomat. Despite all evidence to the contrary, he began to hope that perhaps there was a way out of this that didn't involve him fist-fighting monarchs after all.

He swallowed and said, "He was completely bloody useless, sire. Didn't know one end of a shovel from the other and had a rubbish attitude to boot. Thought he was far too good for the stables. Rude, lazy little git, he was."

"Hey!" Crown Prince Davin protested, sitting up straight. "I'm right here! And I wasn't *that* bad!"

Leopold raised a disbelieving eyebrow at his son. "You really were." He turned his attention back to Mother. "And when did he start to improve?"

"Ah, see, that was when he found out he was the prince, sire."

Leopold gave Mother a subtle nod, and he was encouraged that he was on the right track—although what that track was exactly, he had no clue.

But he did trust Leopold, so he carried on. "Before that, he didn't seem to find much point in anything. He was all about bedding the maids and dodging a day's work. But when he found out, well. It was like he had something to work towards. Picked up his game right quick, he did."

"Exactly," Leopold said. "He was in need of firm direction."

That wasn't anything like what Mother had said, but he nodded anyway.

So did Alexei. "You make a good point, Leopold. Boys need to be told what is good for them."

Leopold turned to Vasily then. "Prince Vasily, your father is correct when he says that being a groom is not a suitable use of your time."

Vasily reared up in his seat like he'd been struck before jutting his chin out in a stubborn gesture that Mother was all too familiar with. "I don't care what's suitable! I'm not leaving!"

Leopold held up both palms. "I'm just saying, your father has a point."

Mother found himself holding his breath.

"Exactly!" Alexei exclaimed, nodding vigorously. "You cannot stay here dallying with horses! You are an embarrassment to the family."

Vasily's face crumpled, and Mother fought back a surge of protectiveness while he took a moment to reconsider his no-punching-the-king decision.

"Alexei." The queen's voice was low and controlled, but there was a hard edge to it. "You will not call Vasily an embarrassment."

Alexei swallowed loudly enough that everyone in the room

heard it. "Of course not, my love," he said quietly, "but you must admit that he is not fulfilling the expectations of his birthright."

Queen Irina waved her hand in a dismissive motion. "So we will find him a suitable role."

Alexei's brow furrowed. "I have offered him a role. He comes home and enters a diplomatic marriage."

Vasily cringed visibly, and Mother squeezed his knee under the table.

Queen Irina, though, tapped a fingertip against her chin. "If Vasily marries, he will have to leave Koroslova."

"Yes?" Alexei spread his hands as if to say *and?*

"So why bring him home to be safe, only to send him away again?" The queen hummed. "Why is it, husband, that you think marriage is the only way Vasily can be useful? And by the by, why have we never appointed an ambassador to Lilleforth? They are a powerful kingdom, and I would think you would want to be on good terms with them."

"I—of course I wish to be on good terms," Alexei said, and Mother took a moment to admire the way the queen had so easily shifted her husband's focus. He wondered if Alexei had even noticed.

"Yes, why haven't we done that before now?" Leopold asked, turning his full attention to Alexei. "I, for one, would welcome a representative living here. It would have to be someone of high status, though, to put paid to the rumours that our kingdoms are at odds. We don't want being appointed as the ambassador to Lilleforth to be perceived as some sort of punishment."

Alexei opened his mouth, but before he could speak, Irina leapt in.

"I agree," she said. "Whoever we post here would need to be personable, of course, as they are the representation of Koroslova. So none of your grumpy generals, husband."

"And it would need to be somebody who was willing to stay indefinitely," Leopold added, sending Vasily a significant look.

Vasily blinked and his defeated expression slowly gave way to a tremulous smile as he sat up straight. "That...sounds perfect for me, actually."

"Of course!" Leopold exclaimed. "A member of the Koroslovan royal family as the ambassador? What could be better? I don't know why I didn't think of it myself. Alexei, you're a genius!"

Irina moved to stand behind Alexei's chair, where she ran her hands over his shoulders in a soothing motion. "My husband is right, of course. Vasily should remain in Lilleforth as an ambassador. The king has spoken!"

The king in question tilted his head back to look at his wife, his brow furrowed. "Have I?"

Mother waited with bated breath to see if Alexei would argue, but then Irina leaned down and whispered something in his ear. He blinked, straightened in his chair, spread his palms on the table, and smiled widely. "I have decided. Vasily, you will remain in Lilleforth as ambassador, a position fitting for a prince."

Mother felt like he'd just watched one of those street performers who started with a handkerchief and somehow, while the audience was distracted, turned it into a rabbit.

It was glorious.

"I—yes," Vasily said. He let out a shaky breath. "And I can stay permanently?"

"Of course," Alexei said, "although your mother and I would appreciate a visit now and then."

Vasily nodded, blinking rapidly, and he looked almost as stunned as Alexei.

Mother wanted nothing more than to pull him into his arms, hold him close, and soothe him with soft kisses—but of course, he couldn't. Vasily's father couldn't know that he and Mother were anything more than friends.

His heart squeezed.

Vasily must have felt the same, casting him a glance that was pure longing. Then he straightened his spine and cleared his throat, and moving slowly, lifted their hands from his knee and set them still clasped on the table, trembling slightly. "You should know," he said, and the tremor in his voice was probably undetectable to anyone except Mother, "that if you had any future plans to marry me off to a princess, you should put them aside."

His father stared at their hands, slowly raising his head until he was looking Vasily in the eye. "What are you saying?"

Vasily held his gaze, unflinching, and said, "I've found someone I love, Father. Mother Jones is the man for me."

Mother thought his heart might burst out of his chest, a mixture of pride and affection filling him to overflowing. Bolstered by Vasily's courage, he lifted their hands and kissed Vasily's knuckles in the ensuing silence.

"But...you are from Koroslova," Alexei said slowly, his brow creased. "Men do not love men in Koroslova."

Queen Irina swept around the table and planted a kiss on Vasily's forehead, and then, to his shock, did the same to Mother. "But we are in Lilleforth, and so Vasily may love who he pleases," she declared, shooting Alexei a look that dared him to argue.

Alexei looked from Vasily to Mother and back at where their hands were joined. "Two men. This makes no sense to me."

"It doesn't have to," Vasily said, and Mother caught a glimpse of his nobility as he looked his father in the eye, unflinching.

Mother had never been prouder.

Alexei turned his attention to Mother. "And you, Mister Jones. You return Vasily's feelings?"

He gave a sharp nod. "Aye," he said roughly.

Alexei regarded him for a long moment. Mother held his gaze, barely daring to breathe, but prepared to challenge the king if it meant protecting Vasily's—*their*—happiness.

The king heaved a sigh and threw his hands up in the air. "We have a saying in the Koroslovan army. What happens away, happens away. It means," he added, "that what Vasily does while he is in Lilleforth is none of my business. And since he will be staying here permanently, I suppose he may do as he pleases."

All the breath whooshed from Mother's lungs, and a weight that he hadn't known he'd been carrying disappeared, just like that.

It was hardly a ringing endorsement, but judging by the way Vasily's face lit up with a smile, it was more than enough for him—and really, that was all that mattered.

Mother found himself blinking back a wet sheen, and he could barely swallow around the lump in his throat as what had just happened hit him.

Vasily was *staying*.

~

"I don't see why we had to stay for dessert," Mother groused as they walked back to their cottage together, but there was no heat in his complaint.

Vasily laughed. "I'm sorry, but I'm the Koroslovan ambassador now. It would have been rude to leave."

"That, and your mum wanted to talk to you, and she doesn't strike me as a woman who takes no for an answer."

Vasily grinned, reaching out and taking Mother's hand. "She's a force of nature but a well-mannered one. She's a..." He paused in thought. "A very heavy thing wrapped in a very soft thing?"

"A cudgel in a wool blanket?" Mother suggested.

Vasily wrinkled his nose. "Maybe? Anyway, it turned out that she and Leo planned that whole thing, did you know? Leo suggested the ambassadorship, but she was the one who knew how to make my father agree."

"Fancy that," Mother said. He couldn't stop smiling, and whenever he looked at Vasily, his heart skipped a beat at the knowledge that, when faced with an impossible choice, Vasily had chosen *him*.

When they reached the cottage, Mother swung Vasily around and backed him against the door. "Have I told you how fine you look, Ambassador?" He didn't give Vasily a chance to answer, instead leaning in and claiming his mouth in a kiss like he'd been wanting to do since Vasily had first stated in a shaking voice that he was staying.

Vasily's lips parted under his, and Mother spent a moment savouring the taste of him, something that he hadn't been sure he'd get to have again. When he pulled back, Vasily's lips were red and kiss-plump and his eyes were dark. He was mouth-watering, and Mother wanted him with an intensity that scared him.

Vasily must have felt the same because he fumbled the door open and dragged Mother inside, settling his hands on Mother's hips and pulling him close before kissing him again, this time with more heat. By the time they parted they were both hard, and desire burned low and hot in Mother's belly.

Wordlessly they stripped out of their clothing and tumbled onto the bed together, and Mother couldn't keep the smile off his face as he pushed Vasily onto his back and lay down beside him, taking time to appreciate all the bare skin and muscle on display. While Vasily looked very nice dressed up in his finery, Mother preferred the real man under the trappings and probably always would.

He propped himself up on one elbow, leaned over, and gave Vasily's braid a gentle tug. "You forgot something." He undid the tie, running his fingers through the hair and easing it free until Vasily was surrounded by a coronet of gold, his wavy locks spread out over his pillow.

"You prefer me undone," Vasily said with a smile.

"I prefer you any way I can have you," Mother corrected.

There didn't seem to be any need for words after that, so Mother let his feelings be known through soft kisses down Vasily's throat and gentle touches before his own desire grew too great to ignore. He rolled them so they were pressed together and rutted against Vasily, the push-pull of their cocks soft and slow and perfect, before finally wrapping a hand around both their lengths and stroking them off until they came, gasping, within seconds of each other.

They lay there, both panting, and Mother closed his eyes, savouring the lazy, just-fucked feeling. He kept them closed when he felt the bed dip and move as Vasily got up and came back with a damp cloth, cleaning up the mess on his belly before letting out a soft sigh.

He did open his eyes then, to find Vasily sitting on the side of the bed staring down at him, his mouth curved into a soft smile. "I love you, Bryn," Vasily said quietly.

Mother's insides flip-flopped pleasantly, and he wondered if he'd ever tire of hearing that. "And I love you." Reaching up, he pulled Vasily down onto the bed and arranged them so he was the big spoon, his arms wrapping around Vasily and holding him firmly in place.

"I'm not going anywhere, Bryn," Vasily said, a hint of laughter in his voice, but he didn't try and escape Mother's grip, and before long his breathing was slow and regular, his body relaxed in sleep.

Mother gave a contented sigh and kissed the back of his neck.

No, Vasily wasn't going anywhere at all.

Epilogue

"Don't fidget, Flick."

"Well, don't make me wear a coronet next time. I swear it's going to fall off."

Leo let out a sigh. "It will if you keep prodding it. Just...sit there and smile. We're almost at the harbour."

Vasily grinned as he listened to the king and his husband bickering in front of him. Since he was here in his role as ambassador to Koroslova and not as a prince, *he* didn't have to deal with a coronet. He only had to wear his formal attire, ride in the procession down to the harbour for the Blessing of the Fleet, and listen to the bishop's interminable droning.

Afterwards, he'd meet up with Mother and they'd wander through the stalls and eat fried dough, and then they'd go and have supper with Mother's parents.

It had taken at least half a dozen visits before Mrs. Jones had stopped curtsying to him, and even then it had only been after that time they'd both gotten tipsy on cheap gin at Rosie's that she'd seemed to relax around him.

Mother's father had merely raised an eyebrow the first time Mother had introduced them and said, "You'd be the lad who can't swim, then?" And then as soon as the weather had warmed up properly, he'd turned up on their doorstep at dawn and proceeded to whisk Vasily down to the beach every single day until he was convinced Vasily wouldn't drown.

Since there were lots of other things Vasily would much rather have been doing at dawn—namely, Mother—he'd tried his hardest to learn the basics, and it had taken less than ten days before Vasily had managed to swim far enough out and back to earn a nod of approval and a slap on the back.

He took the lessons for what they were—a mark of acceptance, a welcome to the family, and a promise that someone cared. And through the summer, he and Mother had spent many pleasant evenings splashing about as he became more accomplished, until he could now swim confidently.

Although he was technically no longer the royal groom, he still spent most of his time in the stables because that was where Mother was, and Vasily would never tire of spending time with him—and it wasn't like anyone was checking on his diplomatic duties anyway.

The procession inched forward slowly, his horse moving in a gentle, rolling rhythm. She was a pale grey, one of his favourites from the stables in Koroslova. His father had gifted her to him when he'd visited his family six months ago. Vasily had gone alone, unsure of his reception when he was on home soil, but his mother had been overjoyed to see him, and while his father, as always, had been more reserved, his gift had gone a long way to telling Vasily without words that the king really did just want his son to be happy.

To his left, Janus muttered, "Could they go any slower? I'm just glad I won't have to sit through another one of these." It turned out that all his mutterings about being too old to run the guard had been more than empty noise. He was stepping down from the position, and Thomas was taking his place. Vasily had no doubt that Thomas would do well—anyone looking at the giant bear of a man would have second thoughts about tackling him, and he'd certainly have no trouble whipping the new recruits into shape.

Vasily scanned the crowd as the horses came to rest at the harbour, and grinned when he saw Mother, half a head taller than everyone else, waving at him. He waved back and as the bishop started to drone on, he closed his eyes and stifled a yawn. Last night they'd stayed awake far too late, still greedy for each other even after a year. Vasily had teased Mother until he was begging before fucking him long and slow, and they'd been so tired that they'd fallen asleep with his cock still lodged in Mother's body like they were two halves of the same person.

He smiled to himself at the thought.

Mother Jones *was* his other half; there was no denying it.

~

"That bishop adds bits every year, I swear," Mother said later, sighing as they walked down to the harbour wall.

"The fair was nice, though." Vasily had taken off his doublet and slung it over his shoulder and was enjoying the cool breeze through his shirt. He was on his second serving of fried dough, and he was seriously considering a third.

They settled on their spot and watched the boats, enjoying the gentle lapping of the water against the stones and the bright blue of the sky, but Vasily couldn't help but feel something was afoot. Mother kept glancing over at him as if he wanted to say something, then closing his mouth again. Vasily wondered if he had powdered sugar on his face, but after surreptitiously running a hand over his cheeks, he was confident that wasn't it.

The next time Mother opened his mouth and hesitated, Vasily reached out and grabbed his hand. "What is it, Bryn?"

It was cheating, he knew, using Mother's real name—but it was also effective. Mother's gaze turned soft, and he gave a wry smile. "Ah well, love. There's no hiding anything from you, is there?" He fished in his pocket and held something out on his palm.

Vasily stared.

Mother ducked his head and ran a hand over the back of his neck. "I don't know how you do it in Koroslova, but it's for a handfasting."

"I know what it is," Vasily said. He picked up the long strip of soft leather, his heart beating faster.

Mother shifted uncomfortably. "You're a prince and I've no right, but I love you, so this is me, asking."

Vasily didn't hesitate. He took Mother's hand and placed it in his own, wrapped the leather loosely around both their wrists, and leaned in to kiss his future husband's palm.

"And this is me, saying yes."

His mouth curved up in a smile that was so wide his cheeks hurt. Mother was his everything, his other half, and he owned Vasily's heart.

And now? He was offering Vasily everything he never thought he'd have.

A happily ever after, with his very own prince among men.

Afterword

Thank you for reading The Stablemaster's Heart. If you enjoyed this book, please consider taking a moment to leave a review on Amazon, Goodreads, or your social media platform of choice.

About the Author

Sarah started life in New Zealand. She came to Australia for a working holiday, loved it, and never left. She lives in Western Australia with her partner, two cats, two dogs and a life-size replica TARDIS.

She spends half her time at a day job and the rest of her time reading and writing about clueless men falling in love, with a dash of humour and spice thrown in along the way.

Her proudest achievements include having adult kids who will still be seen with her in public, the ability to make a decent sourdough loaf, and knowing all the words to Bohemian Rhapsody.

She has co-authored both the Bad Boyfriends, Inc and the Adventures in Aguillon series with Lisa Henry. Socially Orcward, the third book in the Aguillon series, was runner up in the Best Asexual Book category in 2021's Rainbow Awards.

You can follow her on Amazon, Instagram, Goodreads, Facebook and Bookbub. She shares a Facebook group with Lisa Henry and JA Rock, The Book Nook, where you'll find news of latest projects, giveaways, and plenty of pet pictures.

You can find Sarah's website at sarahhoneyauthor.com

Also by Sarah Honey

The King's Delight (Tales of Lilleforth Book 1)
Contractually Yours: A Hot Bite Story

With Lisa Henry

Adventures in Aquillon
Red Heir (Adventures in Aguillon, Book 1)
Elf Defence (Adventures in Aguillon, Book 2)
Socially Orcward (Adventures in Aguillon, Book 3)

Bad Boyfriends, Inc
Awfully Ambrose (Bad Boyfriends, Inc. Book 1)
Horribly Harry (Bad Boyfriends, Inc, Book 2)
Terribly Tristan (Bad Boyfriends, Inc, Book 2)

Standalone
Cool Story, Bro

Printed in Great Britain
by Amazon